Friend of the Devil

A Joth Proctor Fixer Mystery

Books by James V. Irving

Joth Proctor Fixer *series*
Friends Like These
Friend of a Friend
Friend of the Court
Friend of the Devil

Coming Soon!
Friend in the Bullseye

For more information
visit: www.SpeakingVolumes.us

Friend of the Devil

A Joth Proctor Fixer Mystery

James V. Irving

SPEAKING VOLUMES, LLC
NAPLES, FLORIDA
2022

Friend of the Devil

ISBN 978-1-64540-842-0

For my sisters and sisters-in-law:
Marilyn Rasmussen, Carolyn Weiser,
Elizabeth Mathiot, Terry Linderer and Melinda Huff.

Acknowledgments

Thanks again to my agent Nancy Rosenfeld; to Kurt and Erica Mueller at Speaking Volumes; and to my editor, David Tabatsky.

Terri F. Remy, M.D. provided much needed medical guidance and information; Tom McHugh, Howard Melton and my law partner John Kelly weighed in with architectural detail and information about office building construction that I couldn't have done without. The gifts of time and knowledge from these four friends is much appreciated.

Thanks to Steve Kurkjian of the Boston *Globe*. A leading expert on the 1990 Isabella Stewart Gardner heist, Steve generously provided insights that informed my fictional approach to this crime.

Thanks to my publicist, Kyle Durrer, who contributed his technical skill and energy to the marketing of the Joth Proctor series.

Once again, particular thanks to my wife, Cindy.

Chapter One

A Difficult Client

Jimmie Flambeau was a man equally given to the grand gesture and the petty display and both were always the product of careful calculation. The gestures were intended to communicate magnanimity, while the petty displays reminded you of the ruthless edge that was always lurking just beneath the surface. As a full-time lawyer and part-time fixer, now on Jimmie's unofficial payroll, I'd seen quite a lot of both in the short time I'd known him.

My office phone rang on a slow Tuesday morning in mid-September. It was a week past Labor Day and still hot and humid in Arlington, Virginia. Marie had the day off so I picked up.

"Secretary sick today?"

"It's her day off, Jimmie. She's part time."

"Hey, a man like you needs a full-time assistant."

"It's just about money, Jimmie."

"Why don't you see if she'd like to step up to full-time? We'll find a way to cover it."

Jimmie wasn't offering help; he was trying to insinu-ate himself into my operation. When I didn't bite, he chuckled and moved on.

"I got something for you, Proctor. Can you come by?"

"Call me Joth. I'm on a first-name basis with all my clients."

"Whatever."

Jimmie Flambeau was a gambler, a bookie, and a loan shark whose name usually surfaced in any discus-sion of extralegal financial activities in Arlington Coun-ty. Often suspected, to my knowledge he'd never been convicted or even charged with any offense because he knew how to skirt the law, work the edges, and keep his important friends friendly and on a tight leash. I had agreed to handle Jimmie's legal matters in return for his help in quietly solving a career threatening problem for Heather Burke, a friend of mine who was also the county's chief prosecutor. I suspected he'd betrayed my trust, but because I couldn't be sure yet, I felt obligated to uphold my end of the bargain. As a result, I was on a lucrative monthly retainer with the express condition that the assignments were limited to his legitimate business affairs.

Because Flambeau operated on the edge of the law, and often on the wrong side of that line, I was careful to start out slowly, both to demonstrate my independence and because I was suspicious about the sort of legal work he might try to foist on me.

"What you got?"

"Landlord-tenant case. Pretty simple."

"L and T? Commercial or residential?"

"Residential. I've got a few properties in South Arlington. I thought you knew that."

L and T was grubby, street level work, but this sounded legitimate, and I was in no position to turn it down.

"I don't even know where your office is."

He gave me an address on Wilson Boulevard, just a short walk from my humble office.

"Can you be here in ten minutes?"

"Let's make it twenty."

He chuckled again. When Jimmie made that sound, any association with amusement was purely coincidental.

***

As part of Arlington County's commitment to developing a cutting-edge business community, mid-sized office towers had been sprouting up like dandelions throughout the courthouse area. Jimmie's operation was situated on the sixth and top floor of one of them.

"Just off the elevator lobby," he told me. "The sign says Freelance Import and Export."

There was no such business listed on the marquee in the atrium, which showed the entire sixth floor as occupied by a locally prominent law firm. As I stepped out of the elevator, I was greeted by the words *Fuller, Cabot & Dorsey, Attorneys and Counsellors at Law* etched in the glass doors in frosted calligraphy. Behind the doors, the place was humming. A receptionist juggled multiple calls and conservatively dressed men and women on cellphones gestured frantically and scurried across the lobby like well-paid mice hunting cheese in a maze. I had once practiced law in a firm like that. The only time I missed it was when I checked the balance in my bank account.

I found the mahogany door Jimmie mentioned down the hall near the restrooms. I tried the handle: locked. I was about to knock when I heard the bolt spring open, and looking up, I noticed that the entire area outside the door was covered by video surveillance.

I stepped into a cozy, well-lit lobby featuring a reception desk and two upholstered chairs with a table covered with magazines between them. This was a standard business configuration, but the raven-haired beauty behind the reception desk was something else again. She examined me with piercing and unflinching green eyes, and I looked right back. She wore a wedding ring and an ostentatious diamond on the ring finger of her left hand. Women like her don't come cheap.

"I'm here to see Mr. Flambeau."

"You must be Mr. Proctor."

I nodded. Even seated behind a computer monitor it was apparent that she was tall and lean without being slender; a vigorous woman who carried her weight seductively. There was no hint of welcome in her expression or tone. I was sure she'd learned long ago that any display of warmth might be misinterpreted by a man enamored by her beauty and that she could get by just fine without a lot of the social graces the rest of us need to navigate the world.

"Go right in. He's expecting you."

She reached under her desk, and I heard another bolt release. I pushed through the oak-paneled door. As I walked by, I caught a whiff of a scent I recognized: an Irish perfume meant to evoke the energy of the sea. I knew this because it had been Heather's scent back in our days together, although the only hint of the sea she ever felt was the New England saltiness that still clung to me.

Once past reception, the entire character of Jimmie's office suite changed. A broad hallway ran left and right, giving access to a series of empty, glass-walled offices boasting dramatic western views.

Jimmie's newly-coiffed head popped out from an office at the end of the hall.

"Hey, Joth. Come on down."

Stepping into his spacious office, I had a view of an umbrella of leafy green trees that stretched miles into the Virginia countryside. It was a view that rivaled the one that Heather enjoyed from her office on the top floor of the nearby courthouse.

Jimmie took the throne-like chair behind his enormous, ornate desk and gestured me to a modular chair with chrome arm rests across from him. It was not the sort of chair that encouraged long interviews. As I sat down, I took a careful look at the heavy-duty combination safe in the corner. If Jimmie had any compromising material, such as a stolen flash drive with video that could ruin Heather's life and career, that would be where he kept it.

The walls were entirely devoid of decoration except for a small, modestly framed oil painting that hung above the safe. Done in the Impressionist style, it was a portrait of a nattily attired gentleman in a top hat, with a dramatic mustache, a pen in his hand, and his eyes focused on the painter. It struck me as out of place in Jimmie's high tech office. I wondered if he saw himself in this foppish gentleman. If so, it might be a clue as to who Jimmie really was, because both of them looked like a man harboring a dark secret.

Jimmie Flambeau was a small, fit man with thick dark hair, black-framed glasses and a habitually stern expression that changed into apparent good humor at unpredictable intervals. Like the man in the painting, he dressed to be noticed. Just past Labor Day, he wore a white sport coat over a blue silk shirt. A blue handkerchief loosely stuffed in the jacket pocket completed his stylish look.

"How you been?"

He asked as if he really cared, but I knew better. He was a card player looking for tells. He knew I was doing the same thing. He enjoyed that game. It might have been part of the reason he hired me.

"Can't complain. No Felipe?"

Felipe Pasquale had been Jimmie's principal thug since I'd first met him, and Jimmie had recently let him take the heat for a serious crime we both knew he hadn't committed.

"Hey, I told you I'm going legit now. These new betting apps are eating my lunch. I have to diversify. Besides, I don't need muscle anymore. I got you."

I adjusted my weight in the uncomfortable chair.

"You fired him?"

"Hey, we parted ways."

"How did he take it?"

"He wasn't crazy about it, but, hey, I gave him a first-class ticket to San Diego. One way, of course. Probably the only time he's flown first-class in his life."

"San Diego? Is that where he's from?"

"No, but he's got family out there."

"They may not want him back."

"Hey, family has to take you back."

"Not necessarily."

He emitted a burst of laughter as short and abrupt as machine gun fire.

"You're a hard man, Mr. Proctor."

"I'm just careful."

"I know. And thorough. That's why I hired you."

I decided to change the subject.

"That's quite a secretary you have."

"Helen? What you have to know about Helen is that she's trustworthy and discrete. All my people are trustworthy and discrete."

I thought about Felipe. He was as dense as a sycamore, but I was smart enough not to mention that.

"How do you make sure?"

"I'm very careful who I do business with. In Helen's case, I know her husband. Plus, she's only here when I'm here. It's a very part-time gig, but I pay her like it's full-time."

"Is that what keeps her loyal?"

A slightly malicious gleam appeared in his eye.

"It probably works that way in your office, too."

Marie was part-time and loyal, but those were the only similarities between her and Helen and I liked it that way.

"So, what have you got?"

He grinned.

"Don't be so impatient."

"I've got a busy day."

That didn't fool him. But he nodded agreeably and reached out with one of his small, well-manicured hands and pulled a thin file folder in front of him.

"Ish McGriff is his name. Know him?"

"Never heard of him. Should I?"

"I don't think so. He works for the law when he's not sitting out suspensions."

"Cop?"

"No, he's in the sheriff's office. Serving warrants last I heard, but he got in some kind of a scuffle over there. They can't fire him because he's a minority, so every time he screws up, they move him someplace else. You know how that works."

I was tempted to tell him I didn't, but this was not the time to pick a fight.

"The guy rents a little rambler I have in South Arlington."

Jimmie glanced at a two-page document and pushed it across to me. It was a form lease with standard provisions on both sides of the page, printed in a dramatic font designed to lend it credibility.

"I want the guy out. You know how to do that?"

"What's the basis? Is he in default?"

"Default? Christ, the guy hasn't paid his rent on time since he's been there."

"How long is that?"

He glanced at the lease.

"He took possession first of the year. Here's the accounting."

I looked it over. Payments had been sporadic, and McGriff hadn't been current since July.

"You want me to start eviction proceedings?"

"Why do you think I asked you to come over here! Get him the hell out. Today!"

I took another look at the lease. Even a cursory review revealed holes that a sharp lawyer could drive a truck through. That was why I didn't like landlord tenant work. Because of the economic disparity, defaulting tenants could rarely afford the cost of the fight, and landlords, aware of this, often skirted the rules by inserting onerous and even unenforceable provisions. As

I said, grubby work. I wouldn't risk my law license by doing it his way.

"That's not how it works, Jimmie. There's a process . . ."

"I don't like process."

"Then get Felipe back. If you want to go legit, this is how it's done."

"Okay, smart guy, what's the process?"

"We send him a notice and he'll have ten days to pay up or get out."

"Well, this guy's stubborn. He's not gonna pay."

I ignored the comment.

"If he doesn't bring the lease current within ten days, I'll ask the court to evict him."

"How long will that take?"

"It might take a while. The wheels of justice turn slowly."

"Don't give me that crap. I hired you because you're supposed to be the fixer. Well, fix this."

"Which means I do it right."

I glanced through the file to make sure everything I needed was there. It wasn't much.

"Anything else?"

He caught the exasperation in my tone. His expression softened and he spoke as if he'd suddenly remembered his manners.

"I know this is not up to the level of stuff you usually do, but it's part of the package with me. The good stuff will balance it out."

I was afraid that this would prove to be the good stuff.

"I'll be hanging by my phone."

"Just keep me posted, okay?"

Residential landlord-tenant work is not only elementary; it's dull and uninteresting and I resented being asked to do it, but I told him I'd handle it and got up to leave. As I did, I caught another look at the painting above the safe. It occurred to me that I'd seen it some place before.

Chapter Two

Fresh Air

My office was hotter than it was outside, and the stifling atmosphere hovered like a thunder cloud. I stuck my head in Mitch Tressler's office. Mitch was the real estate and trusts and estates attorney I shared the downstairs space with. He looked like a troll in a rented suit, and I knew the heat was worse for him than it was for me. He took his glasses off, glad to see me for a change.

"What's going on?"

"AC's out."

"You talk to DP?"

Mitch put his pencil down.

"I was hoping you would."

Mitch was pompous, lazy, and more than a little bit of a stuffed shirt. He was also as weak and spineless as a nursing infant. While this frustrated me to no end, we had long ago found a way to co-exist.

I shrugged and headed upstairs.

DP Tran was our landlord. Born in Vietnam and raised in Arlington, he was agile and built like a light-weight boxer, with the piercing eyes and closely shaved head I associated with fighters. He ran the Twin Killing Detective Agency from the long, low room that occupied the top floor of the small, cinder block office building he owned. It was like a sauna up there. He was on his knees in the corner, laboring over a mechanical unit. Stripped down to a T-shirt, he looked like he was melting.

"The air conditioner's not working."

"No shit. What do you think I'm doing?"

"Haven't you got a service contract?"

"Does it look like I have a fucking service contract?"

"Well, Mitch is going to be pretty unhappy if you don't do something about it."

He threw down the tool he was working with and glared at me.

"Mitch is a month behind. What he's gonna do? Withhold his rent?"

I took a seat at the oak worktable that ran down the center of the room. I found a clean towel there and tossed it to him. He took a moment to mop up, then bent back to the task.

"He's got a safe in his office."

"Who?"

"Who do you think? Flambeau."

DP adjusted something with a tension wrench and the unit sprang to life. The blast of cool air felt like a re-prieve from hard labor.

"Hallelujah!"

He made several more adjustments, then took a seat on the other side of the table and mopped his bald head with the towel.

"What kind of safe?"

"Sentry."

"How big?"

"I'd guess about two feet tall."

DP nodded as he processed this information. He was a man who enjoyed discussing the intricacies of his business, especially if it might involve one of the delicious little challenges that brought him right to the edge of what the law allowed.

"You think the flash drive's in there?"

"Isn't that why people have safes?"

He was still testy about the AC and probably focused on what a permanent fix would cost. I let him steam a bit, then lost patience.

"What do I do now?"

"It's pretty simple. You gotta get inside the safe."

"Simple? Sounds like a tall order to me."

He looked up at me and grinned.

"I can teach you if you've got the time."

I shook my head for his benefit. Breaking into Flambeau's office was not on my bucket list, but I needed to recover that flash drive and I wanted to keep the topic alive.

"Okay, DP. How am I going to get in there?"

"Security?"

"Looks like there's only one employee and she's part-time."

"Receptionist?"

"Yeah, but she's a hard case."

"She's got to go to lunch sooner or later."

"I'm not sure I'd recommend anybody going in there during working hours."

"Cameras?"

"Yeah. They cover the entrance and there's at least one in the reception area."

"Let's talk about the safe. Did you get the model number?"

"No. I didn't want to look too closely. Jimmie doesn't miss much."

"Combination or key?"

"Combo."

"Number pad or a dial?"

"Dial."

"Can you get a picture?"

"Yeah, I suppose. Why?"

"I've gotten into Sentrys before, but it's good to know exactly what you're up against."

"You really think you can teach me to crack a safe?"

"Get a picture of it, Joth, and we'll take it from there."

DP was not a braggart, but I took this as an idle boost, something to put me off from a project where he didn't see a way through. I went downstairs and got Ish McGriff's Pay-Or-Quit notice out that afternoon.

Chapter Three

Heather Needs Help

I was surprised to find someone in my office when I got in the next morning. When I saw who it was, I shot Marie an extra harsh glare. She just shrugged.

"She says she's your girlfriend."

"I don't have a girlfriend."

"You could certainly do worse!"

I could and I had.

As I entered the room and shut the door, Melanie Freeman looked up from dusting my credenza.

"I'm surprised to see you here, Melanie."

She missed the message conveyed by my tone and expression. Her naïveté and lack of sophistication was part of our problem, but not all of it. She hopped up on the credenza and crossed her ankles with a look of schoolgirl innocence that would have been beguiling if I'd allowed it to be. Melanie was a few years older than me, but the years had merely added a patina of glamour to her once youthful beauty. Her platinum hair had been recently styled, curling up under her ears. Creases and age spots were beginning to mar her skin, but her features—the high cheek bones beneath sparking eyes and the smile of a toothpaste ad—remained lustrous.

"Well, I remember your office from the first time I saw it. I knew it could use a little love."

I knew what she was suggesting, that I could use a little love, perhaps right there on the credenza. She was probably right about that, but not today.

The first time Melanie visited my office was as a criminal defendant in an embezzlement case. She was referred to me by her priest, Father John Tedesco. Money problems had made her reckless. Sometimes, that's all it takes to put a person in jail for a long time. We'd gotten lucky and the charge had been dismissed. Since then, Melanie had redoubled her commitment to the church, and in that way, she bore an unfortunate resemblance to my mother. A lot of good that had done her.

She'd been delighted and grateful when the embezzlement charge was tossed. Maybe too grateful. But I was as lonely and vulnerable as she, and now I was looking for a graceful exit, even as she took the sudden and unexpected intimacy of a recent drunken night as a promise of further commitment.

"I know it's a mess, but I kind of like it that way. I know where everything is."

I looked around at her handiwork: a vase of autumn flowers on either end of the credenza and framed prints of several of DC's familiar marble icons now filled previously vacant wall space. She'd even vacuumed the rug.

"A woman's touch will make a difference with your clients. They'll notice."

The only similarity between most of my clients and Melanie Freeman was that they had made a life-changing mistake. Now she wanted me to make one with her.

"Listen, I've got a client in a few minutes."

This untruth was barely out of my mouth when Marie announced a call: Heather Burke. Melanie's eyebrows shot up and she pouted like a child. Melanie knew exactly who Heather was. She gathered up her things and her dignity and left in a huff without another word. I shut the door behind her and picked up the phone. Heather wasted no time.

"I'm calling about Nicholas Grimes."

I was struck by the stilted formality of her tone but I was unsure what to make of it. It was unusual for Heather to skip the small talk. When she did, it generally meant she was at a low boil about something. The friend in me wanted to commiserate, but the lawyer saw an opportunity.

"Nick Grimes? The guy who drowned himself?"

"You don't believe that, Josh."

"It doesn't matter what I believe. I'm not the Commonwealth's Attorney."

"What about the suicide note?"

So that's what this was about. The same priest who had referred Melanie to me claimed to have found the note on the windshield of his car. Aware that I knew Father John, she'd shared this information with me previously, and we agreed at the time that it didn't add up. I'd never seen the note, but she'd read it to me over the phone at the time, when its lack of verisimilitude was first sinking in.

"Grimes didn't write that note, Heather, and you know it."

"I never said he did."

"Then why are you calling me?"

"Do you want to come by and take a look at it?"

I wondered for a quick moment if this was a ruse to arrange a personal meeting, but I knew I was flattering myself.

"What if I told you I represent Father John?"

She took a moment to process this.

"Do you?"

"Nothing's settled yet."

She sighed.

"He refuses to talk to me. Do you know anything about that?"

"That just means he's not stupid."

"Look Joth, I've got a dead body in the morgue, and I need answers. I'm always ready to talk to him, especially if he has anything to offer."

"He found the suicide note. I'm sure he has plenty to offer."

"I'm going to have to move on this quickly, Joth, so why don't you settle whatever needs to be settled and then we can talk."

"That sounds reasonable."

"Let me know, will you?"

"Anything else?"

"I don't think so."

She hesitated just long enough before saying it to communicate some uncertainty.

"Everything okay at home?"

"Of course. Why shouldn't it be?"

One answer was that the county's most notorious criminal was in a position to blackmail her with a video of her husband and another woman, but she didn't know that, even if she suspected the adultery. I was also confident that she didn't know that the other woman was Sue Crandall, her top assistant. But no matter how much she knew or didn't know, things couldn't be stress-free at home.

"Oh, come on Heather. I'm just making conversation."

"You've never been very good at that."

"One of my many shortcomings."

"Don't be silly."

My social inadequacies were not the reason Heather had dumped me years before, but they hadn't helped. Over the years, our jobs had kept us in regular contact, and to my surprise our post-romance relationship had ripened into one of mutual trust and professional confidence. Because of that, I knew, despite my lingering affection, that this was why she had called.

"I'll get back to you, Heather."

"You always know where to find me."

Chapter Four

Imported Pips

It was raining the next morning. I had barely hung my sport coat on the hook behind my office door when the phone rang. I picked it up and heard the gravelly but amiable tones of another familiar voice: Irish Dan Crowley.

"You staying out of trouble?"

Based on my recent track record, that wasn't a conversational icebreaker, but a serious inquiry.

"Trying to, Dan."

"It always finds you, doesn't it?"

"I'm expecting a change in luck."

"Well, I think I might have something to help."

"Business?"

"Yep. Right up your alley, too."

Dan ran a strip club in Crystal City, called Riding Time, and he had been a client and solid referral source for years. As with Heather, the relationship had matured into a solid friendship.

"One of your girls get herself in trouble?"

"No, this is for a guy I know, a local businessman. He says the feds are sniffing around his business and he wants to head it off before it goes too far."

Mention of the feds always caused my ears to prick up.

"Good friend of yours?"

"Not really. Just a guy who started coming around. You know how it goes. We just started talking and one thing led to another."

It was often that way with Dan. He was not easily troubled by the demands of law or regulations, and he was a sucker for the promise of a sure thing. Occasionally, his antennae went up, and when it did he called me. He'd gotten in too deep with people he'd met around the club before, and when he did, he usually involved me to map his retreat. Perhaps that had happened again.

"Did he pitch you some kind of business idea?"

"Yeah, he did."

"If it's too good to be true . . . you know the rest."

"I call you."

"That's usually a sensible practice."

"Yeah. Think you can come by?"

"What kind of business is it?"

"Maybe we should talk that over when you're here."

I much preferred clients who came to me, but I was in no position to be choosy. And unlike Jimmie Flambeau, Dan was willing to pay the fair costs associated with house calls. I grabbed an umbrella and headed for Crystal City.

It was almost ten in the morning and the "Place," as the regulars called it, was just opening up. The odor of cigarettes and stale beer had become as much a part of the ambiance as the main stage and the much smaller cage in the back. Busboys, waitresses and even dancers moved tables and chairs, cleaned surfaces and swept the heavily scuffed hardwood floors inside the narrow, windowless room.

I was recognized as a friend of Dan's and I made my way to the back with a few nods and no questions asked. Behind the bar at the back of the long room was a metal door with a brass sign reading "No Admittance." I pushed through into Dan's inner sanctum. His little alcove was a trove of gray metal filing cabinets and cardboard boxes that constituted Dan's filing system. He was seated in a swivel chair behind a used oak desk he had bought cheap when the General Services Administration moved out of Crystal City.

He'd been studying a balance sheet, which he folded and dropped into a box by his feet.

"That was prompt."

A smile lit up his big Irish face. I lifted a box from a wooden armchair, put it on the floor and sat down.

"Tell me about your guy."

He folded his hands.

"No hello? No how are you? What's eating you today? Business a little slow?"

"Actually, business is good for a change."

He laughed. I was in a crabby mood and I knew it, so I was happy to have Dan chalk it up to the pressures of a busy practice. I was in a bad mood precisely *because* I was busy. That, and I didn't like my most recent client.

"So, how are you, Joth?"

"Eh, same as always. Tell me about your guy."

Dan blinked his nearsighted eyes and scratched at his bald spot. He owned enough properties and enough small businesses that at any given time he was dealing with half a dozen crises that would drive me to drink, but he had long ago learned to compartmentalize his headaches. This was one of several things I could still learn from Irish Dan.

"My guy?"

He tilted his chair back against the wall and crossed his shoeless feet on the desktop.

"Dapper McNair's his name. Ever hear of him?"

"Dapper McNair? I think I'd remember if I had."

"Yeah. Well, he says he knows you. Or knows your family."

"I doubt it."

27

"Your father was a lawyer in Salem, right? John Proctor?"

He waited for me to nod.

"Yeah, he knows your dad well. Or knew him back in the day. I told him any friend of the Proctors . . ."

I tuned him out at that point. This information didn't exactly set off alarm bells, but I reminded myself to tread carefully.

"Tell me about him."

"Pretty good guy. Big personality. Late-middle age. He's from Massachusetts, I think."

"And now he's in trouble with the law?"

"No, not really. At least not yet. He's afraid he might be getting in a little too deep on something, though."

"What's his business?"

Dan was a big man and growing bigger. His swivel chair squeaked as he swung his feet down.

"He's got an immigration business. He arranges for people from Eastern Europe to come over here and fill certain jobs."

"H-1 visas?"

"Yeah, that's it."

"Last time I looked, an H-1 visa required three things: an American job opportunity that requires specialized knowledge, a bachelor's degree or equivalent in that field, and proof of a lack of qualified American applicants."

"That's right. That's what he does. He matches those jobs with his people."

"So, what's the problem?"

"Well, the feds are asking questions about some of these women."

"Women?"

"Yeah."

He read my face.

"Hey, they're legit, Joth. They have the paperwork."

"You mean they've got their shots?"

"It's not like that."

"And you think that's a legitimate business?"

"Why not? He's filling a need."

"Dan, you aren't involved in any of this stuff, are you?"

"Well sure, how do you think I know him? I took a couple."

"*Took* a couple?"

"Two. They're sisters."

"Dan, don't tell me you hired girls from Eastern Europe to work the pole for you?"

"No! Dapper explained that the jobs have to fit into certain established categories. Just like you said."

"How do you slot them into those categories around here?"

"They aren't going to work here. I got 'em lined up to work over at the sports pub."

"You got them tending bar at your sports pub?"

He waved his hands as if shocked by my lack of sophistication.

"No, no, no. No. One of them is practically a concert level pianist."

"Have you heard her play?"

"Of course."

He gestured toward a rickety upright piano in the back of the room near the cage.

"He sat her down there and she played. That thing hasn't been tuned since the first Bush was president and it still sounded wonderful. He wanted me to give her a gig here, but that really wouldn't fit, would it? That's when we started making plans for the sports pub."

"You can't find an American who plays the piano?"

"I asked him the same thing. We're gonna get a harpsichord. Not many people play the harpsichord. And she's going to play the classics. Brahms and Bach, that stuff. Really upgrade the whole operation."

"What's the other one do?"

"She's a pastry chef."

"A pastry chef at the sports pub? Dan, I've eaten there more times than I'd like to remember. Your idea of high cuisine is a fried baloney and cheddar sandwich."

"No, no."

He waved his hands decisively again.

"We're changing the whole model. You need to meet Dapper. He's showing me some ways to really upgrade my operation."

"Tell me about the girls."

"They're a couple of pips, Joth. They're both actual royalty. Yeah. For real. Descended from the House of Zogu."

"You lost me there."

"The House of Zogu is the hereditary ruling house of Albania. Yvonne would be eleventh in line for the throne."

"What throne? Albania's been a democracy for decades."

"That's right. But that doesn't mean they're not actual royalty."

I was trying my best to take him seriously, but I also knew that Dan wasn't one for practical jokes.

"What are their names?"

"One thing you have to understand, Joth; they don't speak English yet."

"Yet?"

Dan nodded.

"Dapper's taking care of that."

"Berlitz?"

"That's so 20th century. He has them watching American movies around the clock."

"What, like *The Wizard of Oz*?"

"No, he's got them started on the *Star Wars* stuff. You know, get them into the vernacular."

Vernacular. I knew that word didn't come from Dan's rather unimaginative vocabulary.

"What are their names?"

"Yvonne and Eva Wonderlace. A couple of pips, Joth."

"And where do these pips live?"

"I've got 'em stashed in one of my places."

"You've got them living in one of your apartments?"

"In the duplex off Fern Street, yeah. It was empty, so why not?"

"They paying you rent?"

"No. Not until they start working."

"Which they can't do until they learn to speak English."

"They're really coming along, Joth. That *Star Wars*, it's got everything."

"Do me a favor Dan, don't use the word "stashed" when you're talking about someone who might be involved in a crime."

Dan's mouth dropped open as he raised his palms.

"Crime? Who's talking about crime?"

"Tell me about this guy, Dapper."

Dan wet his lips, then leaned forward and folded his hands, nodding to himself as he changed topics.

"Dapper McNair. I don't know his real name. Nice guy, well-dressed, good tipper. Very respectful of the girls. He started coming around enough that I got to know him and after a while, we started talking business. You know how that goes."

"And you said, 'I'll take two'?"

He brought a meaty fist down on the desktop.

"He happened to have these two girls with the skills we were talking about. Said he was trying to place them. We got talking and I began to see how I could use them to change my whole way of doing business over at the sports pub. You get rid of the pool tables and the video games, you change the menu, you upgrade the seating. Voila, it's a whole new place."

Voila. That word didn't come from Dan's vocabulary either and I was ready to bet it didn't come from the two pips.

33

"You realize, Dan, if I represent McNair and you get dragged into it, which you might, I won't be able to represent you."

"Why not?"

"That would be a conflict. You might be a witness. Or worse. Do you see what I'm saying, Dan?"

He scratched one of his oversized ears.

"Okay, Joth. You think this might be a problem for me?"

"Isn't that why you called me? Look Dan, I don't know the details, but it sounds like maybe this guy Dapper is working on the edges of immigration law and using you to do it."

Dan sat for a moment and stewed.

"Well, I don't want that."

"I'm sure you don't. Look, the best thing is probably for me to find him a good lawyer who specializes in this immigration stuff. Then, I'll be around for you if you need me."

"I should have known it was too good to be true. Those two girls . . . a couple of pips."

"Yeah. You want to have this McNair give me a call to set up an appointment?"

Dan's face sagged into an expression of disappointment.

"Do you think you could drop by and see him? He kind of asked me if I could arrange it."

"And you said yes?"

"I was kind of bragging about you."

He looked at his watch and I looked at mine. It was ten thirty.

"He's a late riser. Probably just getting up around now. You can walk to his place from here."

I agreed. If McNair had known my father, it would be best to find out exactly what he knew . . . or thought he knew.

Chapter Five

I Knew Your Father

It was hard for anybody to say no to Irish Dan, and that was particularly true of me. I owed him a lot for the work he sent me over the years, and I liked him immensely. Everybody liked Irish Dan. It was the basis of his business model. Even the girls who worked for Dan regarded him as a cross between a surrogate parent and Santa Claus. I've wished many times that I'd gotten into a business where I could get by on a smile, a handshake, and a generously bestowed favor, but there weren't a lot of people who could pull that off.

Dan scribbled the address on a piece of Riding Time note paper right above the silhouette of an unclothed dancer in a suggestive pose.

"He's right up the street."

"I'll see what I can do."

On my way up 23rd Street, it started to rain again. I should have taken that as a bad sign, but I didn't. I was always prepared to like any friend of Dan's, and that was my first mistake.

McNair was renting a neat gingerbread cottage tucked in among the pop-ups, bungalows and duplexes off Fern Street. It had all the earmarks of a Dan Crowley property: good bones, classic construction details, and badly in need of paint and repair.

I knocked and looked in through one of the two narrow, beveled windowpanes in the top half of the door. No sign of life. I knocked again, louder this time.

"Coming, coming."

Someone could be heard from deep inside. A moment later, a groggy man wearing a light blue terrycloth bathrobe approached, turned the lock on the door and swung it open.

"Coffee's on in the kitchen," he said through a yawn. "Help yourself."

McNair, if that was who this apparition was, turned and headed back to where he'd come from. I accepted his casual offer and made myself a cup of pretty good black coffee and sipped it while I looked around.

By the details of workmanship, I pegged the house as early twentieth century. It was a high-end property as Dan Crowley properties went, featuring a full array of functional kitchen appliances, high ceilings, hardwood floors and the spacious, open kitchen off the entry hall that looked out onto a wrap-around porch. Toward the back, the kitchen opened on a cozy and comfortably furnished living room, where I found a red leather armchair facing a large stone fireplace. As I sat down, my eyes were drawn to an oil painting in a wooden frame that hung over the mantlepiece: a dramatic, windy, and wild autumn landscape done in browns and grays with an otherworldly obelisk standing in the middle distance. It was an eye-catching piece of art, but like the painting in Jimmie's office, it seemed out of place where it was.

I was about to get up and get a better look when McNair, now dressed in carefully pressed blue jeans and an open-neck silk shirt of a color I'd describe as peach, or maybe coral, stepped into the room. I got up and extended my hand.

McNair may have been dapper once upon a time, but the only evidence of it now was a pair of well-scuffed, brown and white saddle shoes. He looked to be a generation older than me. He was painfully thin with the distended belly of a heavy drinker and had wide, high cheek bones in a pale face marked with a network of spidery veins that seemed to radiate from the tip of his nose toward his cheeks. Under a thick mop of rusty hair, I judged him as two or three inches short of my six-foot-one.

Although he had the weak handshake of a man fighting an illness, McNair managed to communicate some of the faded swagger of an ex-athlete gone to seed.

I hoped I wouldn't look like him in 20 years. He held my eyes and engaged me with an amiable smile.

"Joth Proctor, I presume? Dan's friend?"

"Dan's lawyer. Which is why I might not be able to be yours."

"I'm disappointed. Dan speaks highly of you."

I saw that McNair's chestnut hair was really a toupee, or rather a wig, considering its fullness, a chestnut-colored mullet wig. I wondered where you could buy something like that, or who would want one. A vain man, I concluded. Or maybe an insecure one.

"Dan says you might have a legal problem."

He chuckled.

"No. Not a legal problem. Just over-zealous investigators with nothing better to do."

"What do you think a legal problem is?"

"Hadn't thought of it that way."

But he had. Another Irish Dan he was not.

He took a ladder-back chair with his back to the fireplace and got right to the point.

"Tell me why you can't be my lawyer."

"Well, I'm concerned about the eligibility for H-1 visas for the two women Dan is planning to employ."

"Oh no, they're eligible."

"Really? Then why are the feds poking around?"

He sniffed. He didn't like the insinuation.

"No beating around the bush with you."

"That's usually the best approach."

"But you're not my lawyer, so I can't talk turkey with you."

"That is correct, though my purpose here is to help you."

"How you gonna do that?"

"I assume you'd like me to find you a good immigration lawyer."

He nodded, but didn't speak as he lowered his head in thought.

"I've had a few tussles over the years and one thing I've learned about the law is that few things are black and white. I'm a big picture guy. Big ideas, you know? But I'm smart enough to know that if you focus on checking the big boxes, like I do, you can run into snags around the edges."

"That's a sensible conclusion. What boxes have you checked?"

He peered at me with the probing expression of one used to making quick judgments about people. I seemed to pass.

"These two girls are educated in specialized arts. And there's a need."

"There are no American pastry chefs?"

"Not with this kind of cuisine."

"How about the pianist?"

"She's gonna play the harpsichord. How many people you know who can do that?"

"I see. And they each have a bachelor's degree?"

"No, but they have an Albanian equivalent."

"Is this what you call snags around the edges?"

I could see the frustration under his bland expression.

"This won't cost any American a job. That's what really matters. I think most judges will be able to see that."

"What matters is what the U.S. Attorney thinks."

His tone changed as his anger and resentment rose quickly to the surface.

"If he has a brain in his head, he'll see it the same way."

"You make it sound like it'll be easy. You know better than that. That's why we're talking, isn't it?"

He took a breath like a man who had already expended his store of energy.

"Okay. I'm listening."

"I don't have any immigration lawyers in my immediate circle, but I'm sure I can find you one."

"A good one. I don't want some tired old-timer."

I didn't respond and he saw that he'd pushed it too far.

"And your fee?"

41

"No charge. Any friend of Dan's is a friend of mine."

He flashed a money-friendly smile.

"It's good to have friends like you."

"It's better to have friends like Dan."

I got up, and as he stood, I shook the limp hand again.

"Your father's John Proctor?"

"Yes, that's right."

"Lawyer in Salem?"

"That's him."

"I knew him, back in the day."

He looked at me shrewdly and then smiled.

"Tell him I said hello."

"I will."

On the way back to my car, I wondered how long it had been since McNair had seen my father. It was likely more recently than me. Then, I asked myself why Dan had been so insistent about me meeting McNair. It didn't take long to figure it out. Dan's gut told him something wasn't quite right with this guy. As usual, his instincts were sound.

Chapter Six

The Devil's Shield

Father John Tedesco hadn't hired me, but I suspected he would if he knew he was the focus of a criminal investigation. This was not only because I'd successfully represented one of his parishioners in the past, but because I'd had a romantic relationship with his late sister, Jenny. The real question was why he failed to see the predicament he was in. I assumed he had his head stuck in the ground. In my experience, you could often find a priest's head there.

As a lapsed Catholic, I avoided Mass like sin, but I'd never shaken the sense of comfort I felt inside an empty church. I retained a peculiar habit that dated from my teens of stepping into any unlocked Catholic church that I might happen to pass. Especially among older and more traditional churches, an empty nave provides a fuzzy connection to whatever power animates our lives and the silence can create a sense of awe if your mind is open to it. I also wasn't above using this practice to facilitate secular ends, and so it was that Father John Tedesco found me rattling my late brother's rosary beads in the fourth row of his church, St. Carolyn's of Arlington, on that gloomy September afternoon.

Father John moved with such stealth that I didn't hear him approach. When I sensed him, I glanced over to see that he had quietly taken a seat in the pew directly across the aisle from me. He smiled. He was a slight man who looked more fragile in a short-sleeved, Roman-collar shirt and gray flannel pants. His dark hair was starting to recede, and he had a calm and beatific expression on his gentle face. This was his turf, and few things appealed to him more than the possibility of a stray lamb returning to the fold.

"Today's Friday. Are you contemplating the Five Sorrowful Mysteries?"

"I'm a defense lawyer. I've got plenty of sorrowful mysteries of my own."

All Priests maintain a collection of tried-and-true responses to cynical attacks on their faith practices, but Father John appeared hurt.

His expression softened me.

"I was just looking for a place to . . . reflect, I guess."

I sat back in the pew, flexing my aching knees.

"Anything else?"

"You can never tell what insights might filter into your head in a place like this," I said.

"That's true, but the devil can reach you in here just as easily as out on the street."

"Do you believe in that? The devil?"

"You might as well ask me if I believe in God. But no, I don't think of the devil as a tangible being with a forked tail, if that's what you mean."

"What is he, then?"

"The devil is temptation. Which is why our Lord teaches us to pray that we be not led into it."

I had a Pavlovian reaction to the word temptation. It inevitably conjured up an image that recurred with little prompting, and once it lodged in my mind, it tended to hover there:

Heather Burke.

I pushed past it, wondering as I did if this was Father John's way of telling me he knew the real reason I was there in his church. He was a perceptive man in the business of judging people. People like that made me nervous.

"Heather Burke called me about you."

He nodded. He didn't seem surprised.

"And that's why you're here?"

Busted.

"Part of it. She doesn't think Nick Grimes killed himself. And if he didn't, how come you found a suicide note on the windshield of your car?"

His brow furrowed.

"Are you asking for yourself or Ms. Burke?"

"Heather's my friend, but I don't do her legwork."

"She knows I didn't kill Nicholas Grimes."

"She doesn't know anything except that the note was phony. She wants to know who put you up to it and who put it on your car."

"And you'll tell her what I tell you?"

"Not necessarily. Not if you hire me."

"So, that's the ploy? A shakedown?"

"That's right. A $500 retainer puts a pretty hefty buffer between you and Heather Burke."

"$500 is a lot of money for a man in my business."

"It's a lot of money to me, too. I don't need to see it all at once. Just a promise will do. And that promise means you can tell me what happened without worrying that it'll go beyond me."

"In other words, if I hire you, and promise to pay you, what we say is shielded by the attorney-client privilege."

"That's the deal."

"Okay. I'm hiring you. I owe you $500."

He reached across the aisle and we shook on it.

"Fair enough. Now, who wrote that suicide note?"

"A man named Felipe Pasquale."

This information didn't surprise me, and I knew it wouldn't surprise Heather.

"And you know this Felipe Pasquale?"

"Somewhat. I know the man he works for."

"A man named Jimmie Flambeau."

The Father swallowed audibly.

"That's right."

I knew the basis of his relationship with Flambeau, but I wanted to hear him tell me.

"How do you know a man like Jimmie Flambeau?"

"He comes to Mass here."

"Christmas and Easter?"

"Something like that. He's a generous donor."

"How about Pasquale?"

"Never."

"Did Pasquale kill Grimes?"

Father John's face went blank.

"I don't know."

His voice softened, and I detected real uncertainty.

"You didn't ask the question?"

"Pasquale's not the sort of fellow you want to make angry."

"I suppose not. Heather knows Pasquale well enough to know that he didn't write that note."

Father John cocked an eyebrow.

"Heather?"

I ignored the insinuation and he continued.

"Not his style?"

"It's not really anybody's style, is it?"

"I wouldn't know."

"It's not how I look at it, Father. It's the style of someone telling the police that this is not what it seems."

He took a deep breath.

"I hope Miss Burke got that message."

We had finally worked past the preliminaries.

"What happened, John?"

I wanted to make this as personal as possible.

"What happened is fear."

"Did Pasquale threaten you?"

"He didn't have to. He pushed his way into the church office. He had a savage expression on his face, Joth. And I was alone."

"So, he told you he wanted you to draft a note? Did he tell you why?"

"Yes. He told me he wanted to commit suicide and that he needed a note."

"You believed him?"

"Of course not. It was absurd. I didn't know what he was up to, but what choice did I have? I did what he said."

"Did he dictate the note?"

"You know he didn't. He couldn't. He may be illiterate. If not, he's close. He mumbled some melodramatic ideas, some concepts, really. 'I'm so guilty. I feel so bad I can't sleep.' He let me choose the words."

"And so, you wrote something that would satisfy Pasquale while at the same time standing out for its absurdity?"

He nodded.

"That's what I tried to do. Some code, or something, you know? I wanted to leave some sign that this wasn't what it appeared to be."

"I think you did a pretty good job."

"It was a hard line to walk. When I finished the first draft, he made me read it back to him. 'Make it better,' he said. I took another stab at it, added some more of the over-the-top language, but I didn't want to go too far. And that's the genesis of the note."

"Were you worried about Grimes?"

"I knew Pasquale wasn't planning to commit suicide, but I didn't know it had anything to do with Mr. Grimes."

"You were worried?"

"I was worried. Yes. I was worried about his soul."

"Felipe's or the guy he had probably killed?"

Father John pursed his lips and lied.

"It was hard for me to believe he'd really killed somebody."

It was a measure of John's naïveté that he'd drawn this conclusion.

"Then what?"

"He told me to call the police. I should say I'd found the note under the windshield wiper of my car. Then he gave me what I would call a meaningful glance and left."

Father John sighed. His recollection had taken a lot out of him.

"Did he kill Mr. Grimes?" he said. "Pasquale, I mean?"

"Everything points in that direction."

"Do you know why?"

"I have an idea. Do you want to know?"

"Not really. He's on the loose?"

"No. I have every reason to believe he's as far away from here as he can get."

He breathed a sigh of genuine relief.

"And Joth, you'll explain all this to Miss Burke?"

"Yup. As long as she explains the rest of it to me."

We both stood up.

"I hope I'll see you here on Sunday morning."

I nodded at him.

"Have a good day, Father."

Chapter Seven

Call Him Ishmael

I had a game of solitaire open on my computer when Marie buzzed me on the intercom to announce a visitor.

"Ishmael McGriff."

"On the phone?"

"No. He's here in the lobby."

Ish McGriff was the deficient renter Jimmie had asked me to sue. A drop-in by an adverse party was unusual, but a smart lawyer never turns down a shot at free discovery. I shut down the solitaire program and asked Marie to show him in.

Marie held the door and McGriff stepped inside. He stood well over six feet with the imposing frame of an offensive lineman. He wore a ten-gallon hat, which he had to remove to clear the door frame, and a plaid western shirt featuring points above the two front pockets. His sleeves were rolled to the elbows. His name may have been Ishmael, but he displayed an intricate array of tattoos on each arm that were worthy of Queequeg himself. Ish was handsome, with clear, mocha-colored skin and close-cropped black hair. His clothes were neat and clean and he wore the benign expression of an altar boy.

As I got up, McGriff extended his massive, heavily calloused hand to grasp my forearm, forcing me to do the same, so that we shook as if we were brothers in a guild of medieval warriors.

"I'm sorry to disturb you, Mr. Proctor."

"No trouble at all. Please sit down."

As he did, he held up the Pay-or-Quit Notice.

"I got this from the sheriff."

"Yes, I'm sorry, but you're well behind on your rent."

"I know. And I'll pay it when I can. Penalties and interest, too."

"When might that be?"

"I don't know, Mr. Proctor. Since I've come to accept Jesus as my lord and savior, I've been better about things, but I've gotten behind. I know that."

He paused, smiled, and assessed me, then continued.

"I told the girls they have to work, you know, after school and on the weekends. I think Margaret has a line on something at the McDonald's."

"Margaret is your daughter?"

"Yes. She's fifteen, but she'll say she's sixteen to get the job. They know it's important to keep a roof over their heads."

"I see. What about you, Mr. McGriff?"

"Well, since Ellie died, it's been difficult, raising the girls alone. I know we need to get clear of this. I'm just asking for a little bit of time."

McGriff didn't look much older than mid-thirties.

"How old is your other daughter?"

"That's Louisa. She's seventeen."

"You started early."

"I did."

He nodded with an air of piety.

"I was seventeen when I married Ellie."

He hadn't spoken an honest word since showing me the Pay-Or-Quit Notice.

"I'm sorry. Sounds like you've had a tough run."

He flashed a generous smile.

"Well, life's not easy for anybody these days."

"But you skipped over the health problems. There must have been some terrible health problems, no?"

"Well, yeah, Louisa . . ."

Ish looked up at me slowly and after a moment his face brightened into a smile. He shook his head.

"You don't believe any of this."

"Of course not."

"Damn."

"You want to start again?"

He thought for a long moment, then held his hands up, palms open toward me. His voice suddenly lost its ethereal quality.

"I just got started on a new assignment at work. I'm just looking for a little time to put some money together."

"Yeah, I heard you got suspended again."

Now his face clouded.

"You'd have done the same thing as me if your skin was black."

I didn't say anything.

"You know, it's a good job, Mr. Proctor. Pension, benefits."

"You can't have it both ways, Ish. You're going to have to play by their rules or quit."

"I could sue 'em. I've thought about that."

"How hard?"

"That's a tough road, man. I really do support the two girls, you know."

"How about the mom?"

He winced.

"I've never actually been married to either of their moms. They got their girls, but I'm in their lives. Everybody's okay with that as long as I bring a check every month."

"Enough of this. You can't stay there for free."

He snorted his disgust.

"You ought to come see this place. Appliances that don't work, a roof that leaks. Can't something be done about that?"

Jimmie had bought up distressed properties on the cheap and was said to be holding them, waiting for the next wave of development, or the one after that. I knew that Jimmie's idea of holding the properties did not include maintaining them. I had no trouble believing this part of Ish's tale of woe.

"Not by me."

"I spend a lot of my money on upkeep. You think he gives me any credit for that?"

I waited him out.

"I can have it all paid in six months."

"Including interest? Late fees and attorney's fees?"

"Attorney's fees? How much is that?"

"Twenty percent of the unpaid amount."

"Shit. That's steep, Mr. Proctor."

"My client still has to pay the mortgage."

"Yeah, but I'm a solid tenant. He can depend on that. Who knows what kind of deadbeat moves in there if he kicks me out?"

It was an odd encounter. Ish McGriff lied like a midway huckster, but I admired the uninhibited boldness that he married with a wink and a nod manner, as if the whole yarn was part of an entertainment. Maybe this confident rogue deserved a little slack. Besides, I needed to get another look at Jimmie's safe.

"What do you do for a living?"

"I work for the Arlington sheriff."

"Doing what?"

"Right now, I'm in the jail."

Clients of mine were in and out of that jail as if it were a dormitory. It occurred to me that Ish McGriff might be a good man to know.

"Well, let me think about it, Ish. In the meantime, don't get fired. Think you can manage that?"

He smiled the big smile again and relaxed. I was finally speaking his language.

He took a business card from the display on my desk, read it and slipped it into one of his shirt pockets.

"I'm making you a commitment, Mr. Proctor."

"Let me see what I can do."

Chapter Eight

Candid Camera

On my second visit to Jimmie's office, I brought along a file folder holding an unnecessarily thick pile of legal documents. The top few were associated with the McGriff case while the others had been arbitrarily gathered from my cluttered desk.

Helen, the impossibly lovely young lady from my first visit, was behind the reception desk once again. She was dressed as if she were ready for a night on the town, and by the town, I mean Paris.

"Here to see Mr. Flambeau?"

I gave her my most beguiling smile, knowing it wouldn't make a dent, and it didn't.

"Yes. I've got the documents he asked for but I'm afraid my copier's down. Can I ask you to make a set while I'm in there?"

She gave me a scowl worthy of Jimmie himself, but she took the documents from my hand as she passed me through.

Jimmie expected his lawyers to do what they were told and not raise a lot of annoying ethical and social concerns, and he was in a sour mood when I arrived. I read his attitude but instead of adopting a conciliatory approach, I got pugnacious. I often react like that. It's probably why I have so few clients.

"You here about Ish? You get him out?"

"There's a process, Jimmie, I told you that. You don't just go in and put his furniture on the street."

"That's what Felipe would have done."

"And that's why Felipe's in San Diego. Can I get a bottle of water?"

"Christ on a shingle."

He punched the intercom.

"Hey, bring Mr. Hollywood a bottle of water. Helen? Helen! Goddamn it."

He was on his feet in a flash. He pulled open the door and stuck his head into the corridor.

"Helen!"

I heard an equally annoyed voice in the corridor.

"I'm sorry Mr. Flambeau, I'm making copies."

He stepped out into the hall and responded to her sharply. I had already set my phone on the camera function and I took advantage of this distraction to snap several quick shots of the safe and the area surrounding it. Out in the hallway, Helen handed Jimmie a plastic bottle. He slipped back into the room so quietly that I didn't hear him return.

"What are you looking at?"

I thought fast.

"That's an interesting painting," I said.

I pointed to the framed portrait of the man in the top hat that hung above the safe.

"That thing? Nice little picture, isn't it? He said his mom painted it."

"I'd say she's got some potential."

"Yeah? You want to buy it?"

"I don't know. How much?"

"Supposed to be worth at least thirty-four hundred dollars. At least that's what the man says."

"What man?"

Jimmie chuckled.

"I won it playing cards Saturday night. The guy needed three grand to stay in the game. So, I let him put it up. He was trying to draw to a straight and he didn't. I took that thing right off his wall."

We shared a laugh and he tossed a water bottle to me none too delicately. When I snagged it, he snickered and the attention I was paying to his safe was forgotten.

"Hey, Mr. Lacrosse, you still got the hands."

I unscrewed the bottle, took a sip, and put it beside me on the floor. Jimmie put my folder of documents and the stack of copies Helen had brought in on the edge of the desk.

"As I was saying, landlord-tenant law is a process and it's set up to protect the tenant. If you don't like it, call your state rep."

"I've got his number on speed dial."

"I'll bet you do."

I wondered if delegate Zack Everett had done the same thing with Jimmie's number.

"You said ten days and I could get him out."

"No, I said ten days and you can start the court process. I can get DP to serve him, but when it comes up on the court's docket, McGriff can show up and ask for a trial. That'll push it off at least a couple of weeks, maybe more."

"You came here to tell me that?"

"I always like to deliver bad news personally. And alternative suggestions."

"Such as what?"

"He came in yesterday to give me his sob story. Can you give him six months to get his life together? He says he'll bring the lease current."

"He give you that crap about his two kids and the dead wife?"

"Yeah, he did."

"And you believed him?"

"I didn't believe a word."

Jimmie laughed at my unexpected answer.

"So, why do you want to make it easy for him?"

"I want to make it easy for you."

"And how are you gonna do that?"

"Give him six months to pay the full amount, plus penalties, and interest."

"And attorney's fees."

"And attorney's fees."

"What makes you think he'll have the money in six months?"

"I like the way he lies. He's got swag and I'm willing to bet on him. He'll find a way to make enough money . . . if he's motivated."

"Motivated?"

"That's my job. What do you care, so long as he pays?"

Jimmie stared at me in disbelief and threw his head back in laughter.

"Now I've heard it all. You working for him or me?"

"It's a good result for you, Jimmie. It gets you what you want at a low cost and even lower exposure."

He swiveled toward the window, thinking about it. He knew the wisdom of keeping his name out of the court record.

"Okay, but if I do it, you gotta do me a favor."

"Such as?"

"It's your partner, Mitch Tressler."

"What about Mitch?"

Jimmie rubbed his thumb against the tips of two fingers: the universal sign for money. I swallowed. I knew that Mitch had a bit of a gambling problem. The problem was, he liked putting his money down on his *alma mater*, the University of Maryland's basketball team, but the only thing he knew about basketball was that it was good to be tall. But I had no idea that he'd gotten himself hooked up with Jimmie Flambeau.

"Mitch is not my partner."

"You share space with him."

"Yeah, and expenses. But that's it."

"So, this won't be a problem."

"It will be if I don't have someone to share expenses with, Jimmie."

"That'll work out."

"Maybe for you."

"You don't even like the guy, not from what I pick up."

"I'm not bringing a suit against a guy I share space with, Jimmie."

"You're not going to have to sue him, Joth, you know that. It's really just a matter of positioning yourself. You lean on him, and he'll pay."

"I'm not going to do it, Jimmie. Get somebody else."

"Come on. He knows better than to tangle with me . . . or you."

"What if he doesn't?"

"He'll pay. It's what the odds say. I always play the odds."

I decided to change the subject.

"As far as I know, you take bets on anything."

"Sure, but the moneymaker for me is college sports. That's why I've got Mitch as a client."

"And you've got a system all set up?"

"Sure. I know what really matters and I get better information than anybody else."

"How do you do that?"

"Look, there's a line on every game, football or hoops. The oddsmakers, they know the teams, they know strengths and weaknesses and they're pretty accurate. But these athletes are kids between 18 and 22. They're bothered by stuff that's not going to touch a pro. And that's my edge. I keep my ear to the ground. If the point guard's got the flu, I know about it. If the quarterback just got dumped by his girlfriend, I find out about it. If the running back is worried about losing his eligibility, I know it before he does."

"And how do you do that?"

"You build a network at each college where I play heavily."

"You think that's going to determine a game? Whether the quarterback broke up with his girlfriend?"

"You're missing the point Mr. Proctor. No, you see the best team's still gonna win most of the time, but don't forget, I don't care who wins or loses. I care who covers. These things I'm talking about matter. In basketball, it could mean two or three points either way. That's all it takes to shift the play in my favor. And that's what I do. I play the odds. Just like your father did."

That came at me like a sucker punch. I wanted to demand who he'd been talking to, but I wasn't going to ask him directly.

"What about my father?"

"I understand your father was a gambler."

"My father was a small-town lawyer, just like me."

"Ah, but he made his real money at the track."

"He probably lost more money on the horses than he ever won."

"I don't think so, Joth. If you're smart, you make it look that way. You win, you lose, but you cover. The key is to have enough bets out in the right places that you win even when it looks like you're losing."

"Is that how you do it?"

I asked the question with what I hoped was undisguised disgust.

"I don't play the horses."

"Yeah. You've got your own system. You don't need me."

"Look, talk to your boy, Tressler. Explain that I mean business. I've stuck with Mitch for far too long."

Jimmie pulled an accounting out of a drawer, reviewed it, and pushed it toward me.

"Tell him my patience is exhausted and I'm ready to get rough. He doesn't want that. You don't want that. You can help him avoid it."

"Are you going to call Felipe back from San Diego if I don't?"

"I'll tell you what. You take on this little favor and get it done and I'll give Ish the six months. But he better pay."

I was vacillating and it was no use pretending that I wasn't. Jimmie was too shrewd for that and he could read a face.

"Tell me about Mitch."

"It's just debt collection. No human drama."

"A gambling debt?"

"Yeah."

Jimmie looked at me carefully. Gambling debts were not legally enforceable in Virginia; we both knew that. But it didn't mean they weren't collectable. There are a number of reasons a gambler needs to stay in good with his bookie, including a fear of losing his connection. I knew things could go down a lot worse if Jimmie turned Mitch over to someone else. I looked at the accounting.

"Four grand is a lot of money for a guy like Mitch. How long are you going to give him to come up with it?"

"I'll give him till the end of week."

"Today's Tuesday. He can't get you that kind of cash by then."

"He's got a weakness. Everybody's got a weakness. Poke around a little. You'll find it."

Jimmie watched me expectantly, waiting for a counter, but I wasn't going to play that game.

"By Friday, Joth. You get the cash out of him or he's going to get a visit from one of Felipe's friends."

So, that was it. Jimmie had backed me into the role of playing the good cop, set up against a much darker unknown for Mitch.

"Jimmie, there's something else I need to talk to you about."

"What's that?"

"The real reason you told Felipe to get out of town."

"Who've you been talking to?"

"Who do you think? Jimmie, people in authority are going to ask questions. That's their job."

"You need to make them stop."

"That's not my job."

"You represent me, don't you?"

"Not if you killed Nick Grimes. Or told Felipe to do it."

Jimmie's eyes got big.

"You know you're the only person I know who talks to me this way?"

"Isn't that why you hired me?"

He considered my question and nodded.

"I guess it is."

"If I'm Heather Burke, this is what I think: Grimes owed you money. You told Felipe to collect it. Something happened. Grimes said something, Felipe lost his temper, whatever. He panics and ends up drowning Grimes in the river. So, now what? Who did he know that he could put the squeeze on? Who's the weakest link he knows? You got it. He intimidates Father John to come up with that phony suicide note that he thought would protect him. When you got wind of it, you got Felipe out of town."

Jimmie listened like I was telling him a quaint fairytale, and "Grim" it was.

"No, Joth. That's not right. Close, but not right."

"And?"

He chuckled.

"Grimes owed me money, that's no secret. But you're the one who gets credit for collecting it. Yeah. You're the one who turned up that girlfriend in Delaware and that's all it took. He didn't want that to get out, so he paid me."

"And Felipe?"

"I sent Felipe to collect the money. The problem is that he took a shine to that little cutie in Delaware."

"He killed him over a girl?"

"He's got a thing for blondes."

I wasn't sure I believed him, but only because I didn't trust him. The facts rang true. The day before Grimes was killed, Jimmie told me that the banker had paid up. And it wasn't Flambeau's style to kill. It was bad for business to kill off the bettors and debtors that kept his operation thriving.

"He'd kill a man over a girl he didn't even know?"

"Felipe was dangerous. I knew that all along. But I didn't know he was a psychopath. I don't keep a guy like that around. It's bad for business."

"Look, Jimmie, with Felipe gone, this will never be closed. You must know that. People are going to ask questions about you."

"But you can fix that. You can explain it to Ms. Burke."

"You know better than that. If I point the finger at Felipe, the first thing she's going to do is send a pair of investigators around to talk to you."

"She's already done that."

"I see. Did you manage to get officer Kelleher assigned to that one?"

He didn't answer, but he grinned. Officer Christine Kelleher was on Jimmie's payroll and he had probably dictated her report.

His eyebrows arched.

"Burke doesn't believe the Felipe story?"

"I think she probably does. I'm just saying that she may want to use this to get to you."

"That's where you get to help me."

I nodded and thought it through.

"It would be a lot easier if we could give them Felipe."

"He's uh, indisposed."

"You got an address?"

"Joth, do you think I want Felipe telling what he knows to the police?"

"So, that's why Felipe is conveniently out of the way? A man's been killed. Heather might feel compelled to track him down."

"She won't find him."

"You sure about that?"

"Sure enough to bet on it."

I wondered if Felipe was really in San Diego. I also wondered if he was still alive.

"Well, that's what you're doing."

"No, I'm betting on you. Counsellor, your job is to get Burke to like things as they are. I'm sure you can do that."

I probably could. And I'd only be convincing her of the truth. Still, something about it didn't sit right with me.

I said goodbye to Jimmie and took the long route back to my office. Two hours passed on that beautiful September day before I returned. The walk did me good and gave me a chance to sort through some of the things I'd heard from Jimmie and Dapper McNair. My father had been out of my life for years, and now, in a matter of days, two people had brought him up.

I didn't believe in coincidences.

I grew up knowing much less about my dad's business than most of my friends did about their father's work, but from what I'd picked up over the years, I realized there was considerable overlap between his law practice and his gambling habit. Apparently, one fueled the other. Over time, I began to understand that my dad's gambling gains got booked as law firm income, though I didn't understand back then that this kind of creative bookkeeping was against the law. By the time I figured that out, he was long gone.

Chapter Nine

Things that Heather Likes

Jimmie had said something that stuck in my head. He wanted me to get Heather to like things as they are, and he said it as if he thought it would be easy. In Jimmie's transactional world, it probably would be. However, I'd spent several prime years of my life trying to get Heather to like the things I liked, with limited success. She was a refined and sophisticated woman and nobody ever confused me for a man of that stamp. Opposites attract, but only for so long.

I gave her a call as soon as I got back to the office. The quiet, grim tone of her voice alarmed me, and after a few pleasantries, she filled me in.

"Have you heard the news?"

"What news?"

"I've got an opponent."

Commonwealth's Attorney is an elected position in Virginia, and it had been a mark of Heather's success as a lawyer and a politician that she'd run without opposition since her first term. But then people around the county started dying.

"Who?"

"Randy Hamburger."

As I repeated the name, I conjured an image of a puny man with a forceful personality who wore thousand-dollar suits and flaunted a comb-over.

"I wouldn't have guessed him."

Hamburger was big law, and white-collar defense lawyers didn't tend to seek public office on the county level: the cut in pay was too steep. It was a measure of Heather's vulnerability that a lawyer with Hamburger's profile, and money, was stepping up.

"Almost all of his experience is in federal court," I said. "He couldn't find the men's room in our courthouse."

"As long as he can't find the CA's office. It would help a lot if I could get this Grimes mess cleaned up."

"That's why I called. Do you have some time if I drop by?"

Her voice brightened. Heather had a delightful laugh, a ticklish, carefree sound that was contagious and I realized I hadn't heard it in a while.

"No time like the present."

"I'm on the way."

Heather wasn't the kind to look for a scapegoat to pin an inconvenient crime on. She was the rare prosecutor who wanted the truth, no matter what accompanied it.

Because I was acquainted with several of the players who might have been involved in Grimes' death, she knew I could help. What she didn't know was that I represented two of them and as I walked across the parking lot on Courthouse Road, I wasn't sure I'd tell her.

The Commonwealth's Attorney's office occupies much of the top floor of the high-rise Arlington Court house, an ultra-modern facility when it opened in the 1990s. Constant hard use and advances in technology had rendered the building outmoded and tired, but the CA's office remained the crown jewel in the local legal system.

I took the elevator to the top floor. Betty, Heather's long-time gatekeeper, looked up from her computer as I stepped into the office suite. She didn't waste her smile on too many people, but she smiled at me. No matter what was going on in Heather's professional life, my presence was certain to be more benign than almost anybody else who stepped off that elevator.

Betty also may have been the only person in the county who thought Heather had made a mistake years ago when she chose Peter Peacock over me. This was the basis of our continuing relationship. We reaffirmed each other's judgment of people, and quietly shared the conviction that we recognized elemental human truths that Heather's cold-blooded nature sometimes denied.

"Here to see Heather?"

"She's expecting me."

"Did you hear about Hamburger?"

"Yeah, how's she taking it?"

"You know Heather: just another challenge."

"Sure."

She hadn't sounded that way over the phone. And I knew that even Heather could be worn down by the ceaseless friction of stressful events.

"What can I do?"

Betty said the same thing as Heather.

"It would help to get to the bottom of this Grimes mess."

She buzzed, and Heather told her to show me in. She was behind her sleek glass and chrome desk, scratching away with a fountain pen on a white legal pad, but something about her posture and expression made me think this scene had been contrived for my benefit. She gestured toward one of the two armchairs across from her desk and I sat down, using the chance to take stock while she finished whatever she was pretending to do.

Neither Heather nor her office communicated the crisp efficiency I was used to seeing there. She wore a tired, gray pantsuit and her strawberry blonde hair was pulled back in an unkempt bun that showed her gray roots. Her desk and the credenza behind it were cluttered with carelessly strewn files and papers, forming a picture that was anathema to Heather's usual Prussian efficiency.

Suddenly, she emitted a deep sigh and threw the pen down. When she looked up and smiled, I noticed circles under her eyes, which were reddened by a lack of sleep.

"Someone needs to explain what you do to Hamburger. He'd never want this job if he understood the demands."

"He can have it."

Heather had a large office with a spectacular view of the Potomac and the Capital.

"He just wants the view."

"And the prestige."

Hamburger was a sophisticated dealmaker, and his roster of high-income clients included bureaucrats, businessmen, and politicians with household names. Heather, on the other hand, was the consummate administrator, and that's what her job demanded. I hoped the voters would see it that way.

"Come November, I'll be out there knocking on doors for you."

She shifted her eyes.

"We'll talk about that later."

It took a moment to digest this nugget, but I quickly processed the message embedded in her hesitation. It was something I should have realized myself. Hamburger would campaign on one of the oldest themes known to politics: I'm the new sheriff in town and I'm here to clean up the community. Heather's rebuttal wouldn't benefit from an association with someone who knew so many of the recently deceased. My connection to Heather would only reenforce Hamburger's campaign message with the public.

"Shall we talk about Grimes?"

"Isn't that why you're here?"

She pushed an eight-by-ten plastic sleeve with the so-called suicide note inside it across the desk. She'd read it to me over the phone, but I'd never seen it.

The letter had been written on cream colored stationary by what looked to be a fine point blue sharpie. I remembered that Grimes carried a fountain pen, so that was strike one. And the penmanship was good: the kind of steady, unhurried lines that no man contemplating suicide would craft. Then there was the language, the use of florid phrases like *swimming in remorse* and *life partner*.

"Okay. Where do we start?" I said. "This note's a total fraud."

"I was hoping you'd tell me something I don't already know."

"Like . . . who killed him?"

"That would help."

"He still could have killed himself."

Heather could be cagey when it came to internal reports and results gathered by the police, but she tended to let the rules slide when she really needed me.

"We can rule that out."

"Because of this note?"

"No. Because somebody crushed his windpipe."

"He didn't drown?"

"That's what they thought at first. But no. Somebody strangled him."

"Wow."

I took a breath.

"I think you know who killed him, Heather. Felipe Pasquale."

"Flambeau's principal enforcer."

"Not anymore. Not from what I hear, anyway."

"Where did you hear that?"

"I've got better sources than you do."

"If Pasquale killed him, it means Flambeau's behind it."

"It's true that Pasquale worked for Flambeau, but he wasn't a puppet. He had his own motives."

"Such as?"

"Heather, he killed him over a woman. I don't know her name, but you can find out. Grimes kept her in a place he owned in Lewes, Delaware. Pasquale ran into her somewhere and he was smitten."

"What was Pasquale doing in Delaware?"

"Collecting a debt for Flambeau. A legitimate business debt."

"I didn't know Flambeau had any legitimate business."

"You didn't hear this from me, but Grimes needed some cash for the cutie in Lewes. He couldn't get a loan from his own bank and he didn't want to open up his personal dealings and financial status to his rivals in the banking business. He and Flambeau knew each other, and Flambeau offered him a competitive rate with limited security."

"And Pasquale?"

"Pasquale's social life was his own business. It's got nothing to do with Jimmie Flambeau."

"It almost sounds like you're protecting someone."

I shrugged that off. I assumed that her investigators had told her the same things, especially if, as Jimmie had implied, he'd managed to get Christine Kelleher assigned to the task.

"You seem to know a lot about Jimmie Flambeau."

"I'm in the same business as you, Heather. I just line up on the other side of the ball."

"I still need to put it to bed."

I got a tingle when she invoked that image. Old habits die hard.

"It's a police problem now, Heather. You've identified your man. They're the ones who need to find him."

"Do you have any help for me there?"

"I'm afraid not."

"What about that squirrely priest?"

"You mean my client?"

Her neatly plucked eyebrows shot up.

"How come he thinks he needs a lawyer?"

"I think you gave him that idea."

"I just want to know what he knows."

I stood up, walked to the window, and looked out over the community we both lived in. We'd come to a sticking point, and I wanted her to know it.

"Alright. I'll put my cards on the table. Father John wrote the note. Pasquale showed up and put the screws to him. I'm not sure he had blood on his hands, but his manner was even more menacing than usual. Father John was terrified, so he did what Pasquale told him to do. Can't much blame him for that."

"Pasquale made him write it?"

"That's right."

"How did Pasquale choose him?"

"I don't know. I understand that Flambeau attends church there when his sins get too heavy. I imagine Pasquale knew him, and if he did, he knew he was a pushover."

"Not because he writes elegant English?"

I looked again at the ridiculous flowery language of the letter.

"Look, Pasquale's an idiot. A dangerous idiot, but an idiot nonetheless. He probably thought if a dead guy's found in the water, the police will conclude that he drowned. Maybe it'll pass as a suicide. So, what's he do? To a guy with Pasquale's background, who's more credible than a priest?"

"Will Tedesco testify before a grand jury?"

"He'd rather not."

"I'll give him immunity."

"Are you getting dense in your old age? He's scared. He's scared of Pasquale."

"But you tell me Pasquale's disappeared."

"That's what I hear. But Father John has a right to be scared of what his parishioners might think, especially if he's given immunity in a murder investigation."

I'd spoken a little excitedly, and Heather laughed.

"I guess I hadn't thought about that."

"Look, last time I looked, a grand jury investigation is confidential. I'll talk to him about testifying. Maybe."

"I could subpoena him."

"Let me talk to him. He's a simple priest and he's nervous."

"It would help me a lot if I could tie this down."

"That would help all of us. I'll talk to him."

She nodded thoughtfully and I could see that she'd moved on to the next thing. Father John was off the hook.

"Where can I find Pasquale?"

"I can't help you there."

"But you know. Or you know somebody who does."

Jimmie told me he'd flown him to San Diego. I was confident he'd told Kelleher the same thing, and I didn't believe him anyway.

Heather stared at me, still waiting for the answer she wanted.

"No, I don't know anyone who knows."

"You know what I want for my birthday this year?"

"Felipe Pasquale?"

"His head on a platter, if you can arrange it."

"Isn't that what you political types call an October surprise?"

"Except my birthday's in September."

"I know when your birthday is."

"I just want Pasquale in a jail cell before people start voting."

"I'll see what I can do."

I stood up and nodded at her. That was how we said good-bye to each other in the new paradigm. As much as anything else, this was the measure of how things had changed between us. We spoke around the truth and calculated our actions. It was safer this way, but I missed the thrill of our reckless youth and the way we used to connect.

Chapter Ten

Just Helping a Friend

When I got back, Mitch was in his office next to the first-floor conference room. He looked busy for a change, seated in front of his PC with an expression of intense concentration on the soft features of his unshaven face. I knocked on the door jamb and he looked up.

"Air conditioning! Thank you. What did you say to him?"

"Nothing. Some things just take a little time."

He caught something in my tone and took his glasses off to peer at me.

"Like what?"

"Like if you don't get square with Jimmie Flambeau, he can make your life pretty miserable."

"Jimmie Flambeau?"

"He asked me to tell you that."

Mitch studied me for a long moment, then spread his arms to embrace his cramped and disheveled office.

"Things aren't exactly sweet around here. Tell him to get in line."

I sat down in one of the spartan armchairs across from his desk and gave him a moment to think about what he had just said.

"Mitch, that would be a mistake. You know that."

"You working for him now?"

"We're acquainted."

Mitch was angry, and when he got angry, he became irrational.

"You tell that pipsqueak to back off. I can make trouble for him."

"I'm just trying to make it easy for you, Mitch."

His face went crimson, as if he were holding his breath.

"What's he gonna do? Break my fingers?"

I wondered where he had heard that story.

"He might do worse, Mitch."

"What's worse than slamming an old lady's fingers under a piano's keyboard cover?"

"Maybe there's a lesson somewhere in all of this."

The recollection still sickened me, but it served as a reminder of what Flambeau was capable of doing. I knew Mitch would sound less cavalier if he had actually witnessed Flambeau's act of appalling violence, as I had.

"I'm not afraid of him, Joth."

"Mitch, only a foolish man is not afraid of Jimmie Flambeau."

"So, you're working for him now. Is that because you're scared?"

"I'm trying to help you out."

"Yeah, well I don't need your help. If he tries anything, he'll have to answer to Heather Burke! You too, Joth!"

Someday, Flambeau would have to answer to Heather. At least I hoped he would. Until that day, it was a wise man who kept on the right side of both of them.

"It doesn't matter to me, Mitch. I can tell him what you said, and then he'll do whatever he's going to do. Is that what you want?"

"Well, you tell him then."

I got up and left without another word. You can only do so much for people who are too stubborn for their own good. Fortunately, at least for Mitch, I did not do as he suggested. But maybe I did worse.

***

I came in late the next morning after making a stop. I brought in an orange tabby cat with me, and with the unfailing compass of a feline, it quickly found its way to Mitch's office. A few moments later, Mitch was in my doorway with the cat in his arms. His face was full of uncertainty and concern.

"What's Sam doing here?"

I put my pen down and leaned back in my chair.

"I went by your place this morning after you left. I thought you might want to make sure he's alright."

The cat bounded out of Mitch's arms, curled against his legs and purred.

"You took my Sam? How did you . . ."

He didn't finish the thought. He didn't have to. It didn't matter how I'd gotten into his house. What mattered was that I had. When Mitch looked up, his eyes were full of terror.

"You owe Jimmie Flambeau some money. And he wants it. Today."

"I don't even know . . ."

"Four thousand three hundred and twenty dollars."

"I don't have that kind of cash."

"You better find it, Mitch."

"I can't."

"If you don't, the next person to break into your house will be Jimmie. And when he picks Sam up, he's going to sell him to a Chinese restaurant."

"Sam's a her."

"Egg rolls don't have genders, Mitch."

His entire flaccid frame began to shake as he crumbled into a chair and began to sob.

"Don't hurt Sam."

I got up and shut the door. I knew firsthand what Jimmie would do to Mitch if he didn't pay up. My threats were tame in comparison. My only purpose now was to scare him enough so that he would avoid that kind of pain and I had accomplished that. Still, I felt the remorse of a teenage bully who had gone too far.

"Mitch, do you know what Jimmie Flambeau is capable of?"

"I've heard."

"No matter what you've heard, it's worse."

"I don't have four thousand dollars, Joth."

"But you can get it."

"Will he forgive the interest?"

"Are you kidding?"

"I need some time."

"That's over. Today."

I looked at my watch.

"Why don't you take a walk over to the bank? I'll be here when you get back. It'll be good to get this behind you, Mitch."

I wrote down the exact amount on a Post-It note and pushed it across the desk to him.

***

While he was out, I got a call from Sue Crandall, Heather's top assistant. I'd dealt with her on several cases over the years and knew her to be a competent if unimaginative prosecutor as well as a complete pain in the ass. She got right to the point.

"I'm taking the Nicholas Grimes matter to the grand jury. I understand you represent Father John Tedesco?"

This was an unexpected curve ball. While I had operated under the casual assumption that Heather would handle the grand jury herself, I should have known that she would hand it off to one of her deputies as a matter of course. The big dog wouldn't soil her hands with grand jury work. The problem was, I could count on Heather sticking to the script. Sue Crandall was more than capable of pursuing her own agenda if she thought it could preen her prosecutorial feathers, especially if she anticipated the possibility of a new boss after the election.

"That's right."

"I also understand that he's got some information that would point the finger at a guy named Felipe Pasquale?"

"You tell me when you want him, Sue. I'll have him there."

"Good. It shouldn't take too long."

"Sue, Father John's appearing without counsel. He's a simple priest and I want to make sure that everybody in that courtroom sees him that way. Including you."

As she chuckled, I heard an edge of malice.

"Oh sure."

"Yeah. And I haven't sought immunity because it could be hard to explain to his congregation why their priest needed to be insulated from a murder investigation."

"That's your choice. It's not my problem."

"You just make sure he comes out of there looking like the exemplar of Christian virtue that I know him to be. Got that?"

She got it alright, and took the opportunity to remind me about who was in charge of the proceedings.

"I'll ask the questions, Mr. Proctor."

I felt that I'd given her every chance to cooperate with me. It would be just as easy to do it her way.

"Fine, Sue. Just be careful what you ask. Because I don't want to be forced to ask any uncomfortable questions about you and Peter Peacock."

The other end of the line went stone cold silent. When she spoke, her voice was as soft as Mitch Tressler's purring cat.

"I don't see any problem with that. I just want an indictment."

"Me too. So, keep it to the letter Pasquale forced him to write. That's all he knows about and that's all he should be asked about. And while you're at it, make sure Jimmie Flambeau's name stays out of this."

"Jimmie Flambeau? Never heard of him."

Now it was my turn to chuckle maliciously.

"I think we understand each other, Sue."

***

It was late in the day when I heard Mitch return. His eyes were red, and his thinning hair flew in every direction, and it wasn't from the wind. This was a man on the edge.

"You got it?"

"Most of it."

He sat down across from me and took a moment to gather his breath, like a marathoner who just completed a race through the rain. I gave him a minute to settle. He was carrying a heavy manilla business envelope. After mopping his forehead with a red bandana, he opened the envelope and spread the contents across my desk. I separated the bills into stacks of like denominations, then counted it through.

"There's only three thousand eight hundred forty-three here, Mitch. You're four hundred seventy-seven short."

"That's the most I could raise. Can't you see if he'll take that?"

"It'll only make him mad, Mitch. Mad at you and mad at me. That's not good for anybody. Isn't there something else you can try? A relative maybe?"

"This is it!"

He said this with a screech that was painful to hear. I knew Jimmie wouldn't take a dime less than the full amount and arguing the point with him would be worse than futile.

"Where's the cat?"

His eyebrows shot up in alarm.

"Sam? I took her home."

"You sure you can't raise any more cash?"

"This is it. Maybe in a few days. A client owes me some money."

"How much?"

"$500. He says he can pay next week."

I shot him a look of disgust and waited for him to look up and process it. Then, I unlocked and opened my top right desk drawer, where I kept my stash of rainy-day cash. I shrugged. It had rained the day before.

"I'll tell you what I'll do. I'll lend you the difference."

I counted out the $477 Mitch needed to make up the shortfall and threw it onto the stack of bills he'd brought in.

"You pay me back by next Wednesday. No extensions, no exceptions. You got that?"

"Yes. Of course. I'll give you a note."

I thought he was going to get down on his knees.

"I don't need a goddamn note, Mitch. Now, get the hell out of here."

I didn't have to ask him twice. I gathered up the cash, counted it again and put it in the envelope Mitch had brought his portion in. Then, I made a mental note to drop by Jimmie's before the end of the week.

Chapter Eleven

Saint Patrick's Day

DP's private detective license had been revoked several years ago for conduct that almost got him indicted. Its sudden reinstatement in August had been a subject of much discussion and speculation in bar circles and as a result my landlord and sometime collaborator had become busy, proving there's no such thing as bad publicity, certainly not for a private detective.

I knocked and walked in as he looked up from the long worktable where he was puzzling over a cheaply bound volume that looked like the Christmas catalogues that came in the mail every November when I was a kid. I swung around behind him, expecting to see instructions for DIY air conditioner repair. Instead, he was studying the specifications of office safes similar to the one I had seen in Jimmie Flambeau's office.

"He's got his good points, you know."

"What did he give you to drink, Joth? Didn't he terrorize your client and break her fingers?"

"Yeah, but . . ."

I was about to say she was trouble, but the disgust on DP's face stopped me.

"What's in this for you, DP?"

"The public good. I don't like Flambeau."

I sat down and sighed for effect.

"I'm not going to be able to crack that safe, no matter what I learn from that book."

"We'll see."

"Anyway, I got a picture of it."

He smiled. This was the sort of challenge DP lived for.

"Let's take a look."

I pulled up the best photo and handed him my phone and he focused his considerable concentration on it.

"There are others."

He swiped through, looking closely at each photo in the series. Toward the end, he changed his posture, tilted his head, and began stroking his jaw. Then he looked up at me, his face lit with surprise.

"What's this?"

He turned the phone toward me, indicating the small oil painting that hung over Jimmie's safe.

"Something he won playing cards. So he says."

DP used his thumb and forefinger to focus on the object and increase the scale. He tapped his fingers on the table, then looked up at me.

"I don't think so."

"He wins a lot of things playing cards."

He gestured toward the seat beside him. I was curious so I came around the table and sat down. DP's intensity demanded my attention.

"Joth, where did you live in 1990?"

"Salem, Massachusetts. You know that."

"How far is Salem from Boston?"

"Twenty miles, maybe. Why?"

Instead of answering, he twisted the monitor of his PC so we both could see the screen. He plugged something into the search engine and worked through a series of menu items before bringing up an article titled, "The Gardner: the Biggest Art Heist in History."

"The Gardner job?"

"Yeah."

He stroked his chin again, lost in thought. Although the Gardner heist remained the biggest unsolved art theft in history, I was surprised that DP remembered a dramatic caper that had faded like its headlines. I shouldn't have been. His mind was a repository of strange, unusual, and unsolved crimes. I think he half-believed that the mastery of so much minutia and arcane detail would one day reveal a pattern that he, alone, would be able to discern, which would lead to the resolution of decades of related crimes.

I also remembered that infamous night, but for a different reason.

***

On the night of St. Patrick's Day, 1990, I had my first taste of green beer, and like a lot of boys sampling beer for the first time, I drank entirely too much. By midnight, I was hunched over a toilet in our family home on Chestnut Street while my mother alternately soothed and berated me.

"It's a good thing for you that your father's out of town. Are you going to be alright, Joth?"

There would be the devil to pay, and I knew it.

On the same date, and at the same time in nearby Boston, as the last of the holiday revelers were weaving and stumbling down the Fenway, two men dressed as Boston police officers approached the Palace Road entrance to the Isabella Stewart Gardner Museum in the Back Bay section of Boston known as the Fens.

The Gardner collection was housed in a four-story replica of a 15th century Italian palazzo, built by Mrs. Gardner for that purpose. Over the years, this doyen of Boston society out bid leading museums all over the world to develop a collection that was the envy of art lovers everywhere and rivaled that of many prominent civic museums. Throughout the twentieth century, the reputation of the Gardner grew. It was the sort of eccentric, high quality, private museum that made Boston the cultural center that it was.

March 17 was a cold, dry night that year. One of the men dressed as cops rang the museum's bell. The guard manning the security desk, one of a pair of poorly trained and poorly paid part-time workers on the overnight shift, engaged the intercom and asked what they wanted.

"We're responding to a call about a disturbance."

The guard let them in.

Inside, the faux officers coaxed the guard away from the security desk and the museum's panic button and instructed him to summon his partner, who was making the rounds. When the second guard arrived, one of the intruders made an announcement:

"Gentlemen, this is a robbery."

The two security guards were escorted to the basement where their mouths and eyes were covered with duct tape, and they were handcuffed to an exposed pipe. Eighty-one minutes later, thirteen priceless works of art were on the streets of Boston. Among them were Rembrandt's only seascape and one of only thirty-four surviving works by the fabled Dutch master, Johannes Vermeer.

Several hours later, after the morning security crew arrived to discover the still-restrained guards handcuffed in the basement, the Boston police, state police, FBI, and art theft experts from around the world were called in, but it was too late. The trail was already cold. The robbery was never solved and none of the stolen items were recovered or ever seen again.

"I was just a kid, DP. But that heist dominated the news for weeks."

"That's right. A king's ransom in art."

He shook his head, musing.

"Did you ever go there? Before the robbery, I mean?"

I took a breath, calling up a hazy memory.

"Yeah. My dad took me once."

"What did you think?"

"I hated it. That was when I thought I was going to play hockey for the Bruins. There was a pond near our house that used to freeze over in the winter. All the kids were going out to play hockey that day."

I thought back and recalled the familiar names associated with the loot and compared my vague memory to the listing on the website.

"Two oil paintings and a self-portrait by Rembrandt, a Vermeer, five sketches by Degas."

I shook my head. I knew enough to realize that all of these painters resided on the Mount Olympus of the art world.

"And this one, Joth."

DP had scrolled through the photographs of the stolen art that illustrated the article. He'd stopped on a portrait of a dapper, top-hatted man in black, looking wryly at the painter as he wrote in a notebook, a glass of beer on the table in front of him. The caption read: *Chez Tortoni, Edouard Manet*.

He looked again at the photo on my phone and held it up for comparison to the painting on the website.

"Does it look the same?"

"Yeah, so what?"

"The one in Flambeau's office. Does it look like a print?"

I thought back to what I'd seen in Jimmie's office, remembering the brush stroked texture of the surface.

"No, it was an original. He said someone's mother had painted it."

"Someone's mother, huh? That's like saying a monkey at a keyboard wrote *Hamlet*."

DP put his fingertip to his nose and considered the facts as he knew them.

"How big was it?"

I looked again at the picture on the computer monitor. Even the picture of the picture seemed vibrant, the brush strokes loose and energetic.

"I don't know. It was small. Twelve by twelve inches, maybe? But it wasn't square."

He read again from the site.

"*Chez Tortoni* is ten by thirteen. Does that sound about right?"

"Could be. You know a lot about this."

"This is my business."

"Art theft is your business?"

"You know what the reward is for this stuff?"

"No idea."

"Last time I checked, it was ten million dollars."

I chuckled. None of it seemed real and a number like that made it seem less so.

"What are we talking about? He's got a copy by some amateur."

DP shook his head.

"Think about this, Joth. As far as we know, Jimmie Flambeau, a career criminal, a connected guy, has a piece of the Gardner heist."

"And he keeps it on the wall in his office?"

"How many people go there? And how many of the ones that do even remember the Gardner heist?"

I shrugged.

"Isn't that enough to keep us digging?"

That struck home with me. In some significant ways, there wasn't that much difference between DP and me. We were both insatiable about tying up loose ends. At the very least, our mutual curiosity demanded further effort.

I looked again at my phone.

"It looks like it. I agree."

"It looks *just* like it. Where did he say he got it?"

"Playing cards. He says it's worth three thousand four hundred dollars."

"That's an interesting number."

He scrolled down further.

"That's exactly what Mrs. Gardner paid for it. In 1922."

A lot of circumstances were falling into place, like unconnected dots making a visible pattern that seemed to be leading to something significant.

"DP, you don't really think it's the same object, do you?"

"Well, I'm going to find out."

"How are you going to do that?"

He didn't answer, but I could tell by the look on his face that he'd settled on something. He'd convinced himself that this was the real *Chez Tortoni* and he was going to get it.

I walked to the window and looked out on Wilson Boulevard as I chewed a thumbnail. DP Tran was a man who relied on gut instincts. At times, this had led to bad results and earned him a reputation as a man who worked close to the edge, but misfortune had never deterred him. I could only hope he'd gained wisdom from his mistakes.

"What do you think it's worth?"

"Seven figures. Enough to be worth the risk."

I turned and met his eyes. His expression was forceful and without fear. He was as much of a gambler as Jimmie Flambeau, but unlike Flambeau, he played hunches.

"You want that flash drive, don't you?"

"I'd almost forgotten about the flash drive."

"No, you haven't. Look, if you can help me find a way to get me in and out of there safely, I'll crack the safe, grab the flash drive and get the Manet. Who knows what else I might find in that safe?"

"Let me think about it."

"Well, don't take too long."

Chapter Twelve

Like Santa Claus

The next day, and the day after that, I found time to periodically wander up to DP's lair, where we continued to bat around the risk and the rewards of breaking into the office of a hardened criminal with a reputation for using violence as a business tool. The ethical, legal and personal implications were sobering.

It was a compelling topic, but for me, it was hardy more than theoretical chit chat. I assumed DP would soon recognize that the risks outweighed the slim prospect of success, but he believed that the original *Chez Tortoni* was in Jimmie's office, and he could not let it go. I knew DP well enough to see that it was the thrill of the caper that was animating him, even more than any possible reward. In any event, he was all in.

Over the next few days, DP floated several ideas for how to retrieve the painting and I raised common sense objections to them all. We could pull the fire alarm, DP mused, and in the ensuing confusion, he could don a ski mask, slip into Jimmie's space, and grab the Manet, but I pointed out that he might run into the fire marshal on the way out. We agreed that Jimmie was a lone wolf and that we could get him and the lovely Helen out of the office on any number of pretexts, but that left the security cameras. Other suggestions were met with similar sound objections. When I left his office on Thursday evening, I was convinced that this was a problem without a solution.

As Jimmie's Friday afternoon deadline arrived, and I prepared to deliver Mitch's payoff to Flambeau, I found DP in his familiar posture of deep thought, his elbows on the long table, his chin between his hands and his brow furrowed. I asked him if he was still focused on the Manet, though it was obvious that he was.

"I think I've come up with something."

"Something what?"

"A way to get it."

His answer alarmed me.

"Well, you're a magician if you do."

DP looked up at me and grinned. He liked to be seen as a miracle worker and I had inadvertently encouraged him.

"No sense in us both going in. You'd just be in the way. Plus, I need you on the outside."

He had already moved from concept to plan. As he spoke, he unrolled a spool of architect's drawings and laid them out flat on top of the worktable.

"What's this?"

"The is the sixth floor of Jimmie's office building. Let's take a look."

The reality of what we were contemplating struck me all over again. I sucked in some air and took a moment to orient myself with the diagram. DP turned it so that the axis of the drawing ran north and south. Then, he moved his finger to the northwest corner.

"This is Flambeau's office?"

"Yes. The corner office."

DP leaned back and put a finger to his lips. After a moment of consideration, he placed a finger on the ruler-straight blue line that represented the wall separating Jimmie's office from the adjacent office suite.

"So, this over here is Dewey, Cheatum, and Howe?"

He tapped the part that directly abutted Flambeau's office.

"Fuller, Cabot & Dorsey, I believe."

"The law firm whose space abuts his?"

"Right. Is that important?"

"If we can get into it, after hours, sure."

"I'm not following you."

"Let me see your phone again."

I handed it to him, and he quickly accessed the series of photos I had hurriedly snapped during my last visit to Jimmie's office.

"Take a look at this one."

The photo caught the wall behind the safe and part of the ceiling.

"Acoustic tiles in a drop ceiling. These pop right out, don't they?"

I glanced up to the unfinished, beamy space above us. But I had started out in a big firm, and had some familiarity with modern office suite construction.

"Probably."

"It looks like it to me. And this is the top floor in the building."

"That's right."

"So, above the ceiling is a crawl space that allows maintenance people to access the duct systems for heat and AC."

I began to see where he was headed.

"If you can get into the crawl space . . ."

"Merry Christmas?"

"Almost."

"Right. I work my way over until I'm above Flambeau's space, then drop right in like Santa Claus."

He trailed his finger back over the floor plan and tapped the end office in the Fuller, Cabot & Dorsey space.

"I'm guessing they have drop down ceiling tiles, too. If I can get into the law firm at the right time of day, I can get into the ceiling."

I imagined him up there, small, spry and agile.

I looked at DP and shook my head.

"That won't work. The ceiling grid is designed to support the tiles, not a man's weight. Not even one as light as you."

"I already thought of that, Joth."

DP turned the pencil point down and circled the conference room and the offices at the end of the law firm space.

"Until last spring, this was occupied by a medical practice. When they moved out, the law firm expanded into their space."

"So?"

"That means they had a reinforced ceiling structure to support the equipment of a medical practice. It'll take my weight and a lot more."

I came up with another sensible objection.

"There'll be sheetrock separating the two office suites. The building code requires it."

"Yes, but I can get through that with a box cutter. You follow?"

I squirmed in my seat.

"Yes, I do, and I see a lot of problems."

"Such as?"

"DP, it might not be that simple. We don't know what we could be getting into. Jimmie's entrance and reception area are under video surveillance. I assume his private office is, too."

I could see that DP had already thought through that possibility.

"I don't think so. He probably figures that the outside cameras make him secure. And who knows what goes on inside Jimmie's inner sanctum? People like him don't usually want that on film."

Jimmie's inner office was where the bets went down and the money changed hands. DP was right on that point.

"Can you get back in there and get another look?"

I had Mitch's payment to deliver.

"I'm sure I can."

The plan was beginning to sound all too real . . . and all too frightening.

"What about the secretary?"

"You said she's only there if he's there."

"That's what he told me."

"So, all we have to do is get him out of the way."

I took a dramatic, deep breath to make sure that DP received a tangible sign of my concern. Then, I reminded him of the obvious.

"It's not that simple."

"If this sort of thing was simple, Joth, the Gardner would have had that art back years ago."

I needed to think about it, and DP gave me time. It was risky, but it could work. I knew that. And if it did, and if DP could get into the safe, and if the incriminating flash drive was in the safe, Heather's problems would be reduced to a bad marriage and a nasty re-election campaign. Those would be a handful for anyone, and I hoped I might help her get through them.

"Look at it this way, Joth. He's got a flash drive with a video that will ruin Heather Burke's career. I live in this county, too, you know. I want to save the career and reputation of an excellent public servant."

"How long did it take you to come up with that?"

"I thought it would shut you up."

I laughed.

"Okay, so what's the next step?"

DP tapped at the floor plan and the office of the lawyer in the corner of the Fuller space.

"I'm going to find out whose office this is."

"Then what?"

"Let me think about it."

"Okay."

There was nothing left to say.

***

I went downstairs and called Jimmie's office to see if he was in and if he had time to see me. Helen took a moment to check and then answered yes to both questions. Ten minutes later, I heard the bolt drop as I approached Jimmie's outer office door. I delayed a moment to comb my fingers through my unkempt hair, using that series of gestures to cover the good look I got at the security camera pointed down at me. I figured any inside camera would be on the same system and of a similar style and placement.

Helen was used to men staring at her and her technique for combatting this nuisance was to minimize eye contact with riffraff like me. That gave me another opportunity to study the security layout as she finished whatever she was doing at the computer. My assumption was correct. There were two closed-circuit cameras in the reception area, of the same make and style as the one covering the entrance.

She looked up.

"Here to see Mr. Flambeau?"

"That's right."

She buzzed me in.

"You know the way."

Jimmie stood up when I walked into his office, greeting me with a broad and apparently sincere smile. For a guy with a reputation for never smiling, I was getting a lot of that from him. He gave me the impression that I was growing on him, but I knew Jimmie too well to trust appearances.

"Today's D-day for Mitch."

"Why do you think I'm here?"

I tossed the envelope on his desk and sat down. Jimmie reacted like a hungry man attacking a Big Mac. He pulled open the envelope and started counting while I systematically studied the ceiling and walls. There were no cameras. The ceiling was composed of acoustic tiles that looked to be about two feet by four feet each, just as DP had assumed. The panels were supported by a grid constructed of flat, gray metal.

Then, I looked at DP's proposed landing zone. Most of Flambeau's furniture looked solid, including a mostly empty bookcase built into the wall, which could conveniently serve as a ladder.

DP's plan just might work.

After making a mental note of this, I used the opportunity to take a closer look at the painting hanging above the safe. The frame was simple, probably cheap, but the painting in the frame was not. To my uneducated eye, the whirlwind of intricate brush strokes seemed masterful and the blending of the colors was stunning. The artist had produced the miraculous effect of capturing light from the window and diffused it through the glass of beer on the table like a prism. Clearly, this was not the work of an amateur.

Jimmie counted his money with the painstaking care of a man who enjoyed his work, separating the bills in my carefully constructed stacks of like denominations and recounting them. The bills Mitch obtained from the bank were crisp twenties and fifties. The ones pulled from my stash, or the corners of Mitch's office or pants pockets, were crumpled, folded and typically of smaller denominations. Jimmie took each of the greasy bills between his fingers and rubbed them. I thought for a moment he was looking for counterfeits, but then I realized that he wouldn't waste time on smaller bills and ignore the crisp larger denomination if that was his purpose. Like a stereotypical miser, Jimmie liked the feel of what was literally filthy lucre.

"All there. To the dollar."

He held a stained and crumpled five up to the light.

"It looks like Mitch dug pretty deep to find enough."

"He did."

"Did you have to push him?"

"Yes, I did."

"He's probably a little afraid of you."

I wanted to tell him who Mitch really feared but perpetuating the idea of me as a physically intimidating figure seemed to be the better play.

"A little bit, maybe."

"You see how easy it is?'

And then I saw that I had made a mistake.

"Jimmie, my commitment to you was to perform legal services. Legitimate legal work. Don't get the idea that I'm going to strong-arm anybody."

"It's simpler this way."

I got up.

"Find yourself another boy."

"Wait a minute."

He kneaded his top lip between his teeth.

"We'll do it your way."

"I don't like being tested."

Jimmie glared at me.

"I imagine you're used to it."

"If I was willing to put up with crap like that, I'd be in a corner office at a big firm."

He took a moment to stroke his chin.

"Alright, see you later, tough guy."

I felt as grimy as the greasiest dollar bill I had delivered. I went home and took a shower and the rest of the day off.

Chapter Thirteen

Valentine's Day in September

I could feel a touch of autumn in the air. The first call I got that morning came in just before noon. It was Heather and she sounded cheerful for a change.

"Don't you have a birthday coming up?"

I was surprised she called, but not that she remembered. We were born on the same day, one year apart, a coincidence that seemed full of cosmic significance when we were in love.

I wasn't sure if Heather realized that her husband, Peter, was having an affair with her top assistant prosecutor. While things couldn't be too cozy around the house, I also didn't know how much Heather would put up with for the sake of her kids or public perception, especially now, when she was running for reelection.

"Tomorrow, I think."

"Are you doing anything?"

Heather was a subtle and cunning litigator and when she wore her lawyer hat, nothing came out of her mouth by accident. But on a personal level, she was different. At least she had been, once upon a time.

"Nothing concrete," I said.

I wanted to be cautious, unsure where she was headed.

"Buy you a drink?"

I felt a surge of heat in my gut and a chill up my spine. The invitation was sudden and unexpected and her motive was shrouded by the flatness of her tone. I wondered what Peter would think about that. Maybe he wouldn't care. Or maybe that was wishful thinking.

"Cup of coffee, maybe?"

She paused and seemed to consider.

"That works. Willard's at two?"

Willard's was a coffee bar a few blocks from my office. It was also a government-owned safe house where Heather periodically turned the screws on reluctant witnesses and wavering defendants. Somehow, her selection of this familiar locale put me more at ease than if she had suggested meeting at a bar.

"Okay. See you there."

It rained the next day, a stiff and steady soaker that began with rush hour and lasted all day. It was a measure of my distraction that I came to work dressed in a Harris Tweed sport coat over a cashmere sweater, but without a raincoat or umbrella. Just before two, with sheets of rain battering my windows, I was reduced to asking Mitch for a loan of whatever foul weather gear he kept in his rat trap of a closet. What I got was a tan trench coat that was too short and not big enough to accommodate my broad shoulders. I took it anyway and pulled the lapels together against the blustery weather as I hurried over to Willard's.

Willard's was a dim place even on the brightest day, but on our rain-soaked birthday it was dark and empty, and the sense of cheerlessness was only broken by a familiar nod from Raighne Youngblood, working behind the bar.

"Coffee?"

"I'm waiting for someone."

I didn't have to wait long. Heather stepped inside, dripping rainwater from a Prussian blue and white anorak. Backlit from the street, she looked like the Virgin Mary as she pulled the hood away from her still lovely face.

"Sorry I'm late."

"I was early."

I stood as she joined me at the table I'd selected. As she sat down across from me, Raighne was already pulling her standard order together.

"Black coffee," I said.

He acknowledged me with a nod and got back to work.

"Happy birthday, Joth."

"To you, too. How old are we?"

She laughed, displaying perfect teeth in her perfectly shaped smile.

"I'll always be a year younger than you."

Raighne placed a carafe of hot water and a ceramic mug with a tea bag in it in front of Heather. I blew on my coffee, and she dithered until Raighne moved away. Then, she got right to the point, which was not her habitual approach.

"I brought you something."

I hadn't been so thoughtful.

"I hope not."

"It's not much. Just something I found."

She reached into her purse and took out an oddly shaped object made of red construction paper. I recognized it as soon as she laid it out in front of us. One half of a torn valentine. I studied it for a moment, then took out my wallet and pulled out the other half and laid it next to hers. Her half was pristine, while mine was tattered and faded, but they fit together like puzzle pieces.

"I'm surprised you kept it," I said.

"I found it in a book."

"What book?"

"*Walden.*"

We'd broken up on Valentine's Day a decade ago.

117

"Didn't I give that to you?"

"Yes. And the valentine."

At the end of that brief encounter, I'd torn the valentine in two and given her one jagged half. The other had resided in my wallet ever since.

"I used it for a bookmark. Never finished the book."

"You wouldn't like it."

"I'm ready to give it another try."

It?

I looked at the tattered valentine, the two pieces so differently preserved.

"What are we going to do with it?"

"One of us should keep it."

"You keep it, Heather. I gave it to you."

I was glad to get it out of my wallet. Years of looking at it had not done me any good.

She'd come armed with a single conversation starter and from there, the talk flagged and drifted into awkwardness. I looked at my watch.

"I've got a client at three," I said.

She didn't believe me, but it was just as well. As I got up to go, I thought about her comment about giving it another try. A woman as hard-headed and practical as Heather was never going to embrace the message of *Walden* and I suppose I realized that at the time. I assumed she was hinting at giving our relationship another try, but that was not a question I was prepared to entertain.

Walking back in what had become a steady drizzle, I realized, regretfully, that we'd moved on from what we once had all those years ago. We'd become something different: trusted friends and confidants, and my instincts told me that a renewed intimacy and the complicated intensity that would entail would spoil all that we'd built in the years since.

Surely she wasn't the same person she'd been. I knew I wasn't and that I would likely disappoint her. It was Heather who had taught me to always trust my instincts. I needed time to understand whether a renewed romance would be worth the price, but I doubted it could work.

I spent the rest of my birthday alone. When I ran out of work to distract me, I got in my car and drove out to Great Fall. The rain had stopped and I parked in the nearly empty north lot. Walking toward the overlook, I noticed that the trees along the Potomac were showing the first traces of yellow and red. Fall was coming. At the overlook, I watched the white water rage through the steep river gorge. It was a reminder that time passes, pushing everything with it. The river rolls, day after day, but the content of the river is always different. It was much the same with people.

I woke up in the middle of the night with an answer. It was difficult to face, and it wasn't the answer I wanted. It was easier for me to be the victim, the man scorned. More than that, I knew I wasn't worthy of Heather. I'd killed a man and although I'd managed to keep it quiet so far, she was the county's chief prosecutor. She'd learn about it someday, and then what? I wasn't willing to bring her down with me.

Chapter Fourteen

DP Maps the Attack

Several days and a weekend went by, and whenever I saw DP in the hallway, he passed me without a word, his brow furrowed in concentration. And then one day, he summoned me up to his office. He was smiling and relaxed as if he'd shaken an illness that had consumed him for a week.

Following his lead, I sat across from him at the long, oak worktable. The floor plan of the top floor of Jimmie's office building was spread out on the table between us, its four corners held down by a tattered Vietnamese-English dictionary, a grimy socket wrench, a box compass, and a heavy paperweight depicting Buddha, seated with his right hand raised and facing toward me. It felt like he was delivering a warning. Nothing was holding down my doubts and both DP's manner and his formal staking out of the plans made me nervous. I saw that playtime was over and we were committing to the real thing.

"You aren't really going to do this?"

DP had tunnel vision whenever he locked in on a plan.

"That's what we agreed on, Joth."

"There's got to be a better way."

"Aren't we in a little too deep to be worrying about that?"

When I didn't answer, he looked up, then threw his pencil down with a deep sigh.

"You know what Flambeau's going to do with that flash drive? Joth, this is a bad guy. He is a criminal, and the law can't touch him as it is. With the flash drive, he's capable of anything. We're the only ones who can do something about that. If we're willing."

The flash drive had seemed forgotten when DP was dreaming up this scheme, but he loved to wear the white hat and he usually found a way to look at a problem from that perspective. We were contemplating a crime and courting all the personal and professional risk associated with that conduct. Somewhere inside my head, red flags were waving, but something else in me was willing to set caution aside, to follow this dangerous path to the end.

"You know, you can sound like a very reasonable man when you put your mind to it. How do we get around the breaking and entering part?"

"We're preventing a bigger crime; preventing him from using it to harm someone you care about. We've covered all that."

Risk was never part of DP's value calculation, but I did not share his optimism and he could read this on my face.

"Or we could drop the whole thing," he said.

I suppose that was what I wanted to hear him say. He'd called my bluff, but we both knew I couldn't walk away from it at this point.

"No. I've been willing to do stupid things for Heather for a long time. I'm not going to stop now."

Especially now. I paused and turned to the other aspect of it.

"What about the Manet, if that's what it is? What do we do with it once we've got it?"

"You let me worry about that little detail."

"A little detail? We can't sell it."

"Not on the open market, no."

I could see that DP had already thought this problem through.

"It's still red hot. You think you can fence something like that?"

He winked at me.

"Whatever we get, we'll split it. If we can't do anything with it, we'll return it to the museum."

"That part's okay with me."

I asked the money question because I wanted his re-action, and I could see that it wasn't the money that was motivating him. It was the thrill of the high wire, the chance to risk it all. That's what appealed to DP. He was a good friend, but a dangerous one.

"Just be careful, okay?"

"I'm always careful."

I wanted to ask him how careful he'd been when he concocted the caper that had cost him his detective's license, but I bit my tongue. I could only hope that he'd learned from that ugly experience.

He unrolled another tube of floor plans on the table and flattened it with his palms, then turned it so that it's geographical coordinates tracked true north and south. As he did, I saw that it was the floor plan for Fuller, Cabot & Dorsey, the law firm whose space abutted Flambeau's. I wondered where he got them, but I knew better than to ask. DP liked to maintain an aura of mystery, and I really didn't want to know.

After weighing down the four corners of the sheet, he ran his index finger across the plan, pointing out the elevator lobby, the reception desk, and the wall that separated the law firm from Flambeau's space. He allowed me time to acquaint myself with the set up, then tapped his finger on the northwestern edge of the Fuller space.

"Jimmie has a corner office and it's at the end of his space. The Fuller firm is on the other side of his wall."

He picked up a pencil and drew an X on the floor plan.

"On the Fuller side, the corridor dead-ends here. This is the old medical office. There are two lawyers' offices on the window side and a pair of interior offices across the corridor."

Following the tip of the pencil, I also saw that a conference room and a storage closet separated these two lawyer's offices from the rest of the firm.

"This is where we need to operate."

There was a name printed across the last office in the Fuller space; the lawyer whose office butted up against the common wall. I tilted my head and read it:

"Grace Patrick."

"You know her?"

"I know who she is, a junior partner in the firm's land use practice."

DP rubbed his poorly shaved jaw line.

"I checked her out. From what I hear, she's reliably gone by five-thirty every night."

I didn't share his willingness to accept risk.

"What's 'reliably' mean?"

"If we pick a Friday, we'll be alright. If she's gone, she's not coming back. If she's there, we abort and just leave the way we came in."

I traced my finger to the office of Patrick's neighbor.

"We're going to have to make sure this office is empty, too."

DP read the name printed across the square that marked her office.

"Emily Davison."

He looked up at me.

"You know anything about her?"

"Yeah. Immigration lawyer."

"Really? I didn't know Fuller had an immigration practice."

"They didn't. They poached her from another firm this summer. They signed her up to build one for them."

As I spoke, a light bulb went off in my head. A lateral attorney starting a new practice group at an established firm was under immediate pressure to produce. I remembered Irish Dan's friend, Dapper McNair. He'd asked me to connect him to an immigration lawyer.

"I think I can take care of her."

"Good. Here's the lay-out. The cleaning crews comes in between six-thirty and seven. They're usually punctual but almost never early. The reception desk closes at six, but the cleaning crew has their own keys. If we get in there just before six, I figure we've got an hour."

"That doesn't sound like an hour to me."

"I think I can make sure they're on the late side."

"Is that enough time?"

"If I can't get in that safe in ten minutes, I can't get in it at all."

That raised the big question.

"How are we getting into the law firm?"

"The best way, Joth. We just walk in."

DP folded his hands and adopted a professorial attitude.

"The cleaning crew wears green jumpsuits. I can get us a couple, and a laundry cart filled with cleaning supplies. We move fast but not too fast. Confident, you know? Like we belong there."

"People are going to be suspicious."

"Not a chance. Clean-up crews are faceless people. We'll have ball caps on and keep our heads down."

I took a breath. The mental picture agonized me.

"Okay. Then what?"

"Once we get past the reception desk, we move straight down the corridor to these two offices and start cleaning. From there, it's up to me. I'll pop up a ceiling tile. You hoist me up. I'll carry a flashlight and a boxcutter. Once I'm up there, I'll replace the tile and you vacuum up any debris. Anybody comes by, you're cleaning."

"What about you?"

"The building code requires the studs in the fire wall between offices to be sixteen inches apart. I'll use the box cutter to slice through the sheetrock between the studs and squeeze through. Once I do that, I'll be right above Jimmie's office."

"There's a bookcase set into Flambeau's wall. You'll be able to use it to climb down."

DP nodded.

"Good information."

"We'll need to make sure he's out of there."

"I'll leave that to you," said DP.

He took a heavy breath.

"I'll lift the tile, drop down and open the safe. If the flash drive is in there, I'll replace it with a blank flash drive, grab the Manet, sweep up any debris I knocked loose and get the hell out of there."

I processed this with a grim nod.

"When do you want to do this?"

"Sooner the better. We've got three days until Friday. I can be ready by then."

"That doesn't leave much time."

"We don't need much time. All you need to do is arrange to get that new lawyer, Davison, out of there and account for Jimmie."

DP looked at me expectantly as I thought it through. Once again, I measured the terrible risk against the possible gain. Thinking it through coldly, it made no sense to risk my freedom for a woman married to another man, but I found myself fired up by DP's zest for a high risk caper, and his willingness to stick his neck out. The Gardner thieves must have felt a similar rush on that St. Patrick's Day night so many years before.

"Alright. I'm in. Friday it is."

Chapter Fifteen

Two Unhappy Women

On Thursday afternoon, I called Fuller, Cabot & Dorsey and asked for Emily Davison. The receptionist put the call through, and a woman's gruff, unfriendly voice answered.

"Emily Davison."

"Emily, this is Joth Proctor. I've got a law practice just down the street from you."

"Yes?"

I could tell she knew who I was, and she sounded horrified to be talking to me. It's a small bar and rumors breed like rabbits.

"I've got a client who needs a good immigration lawyer. Several people have told me to call you."

The promise of business melted her concerns.

"I hope I am. What sort of case is it?"

"My client's being investigated by the U.S. Attorney in Alexandria for possible immigration fraud. He needs somebody to head off the problem."

"What's his name?"

I gave her McNair's name.

"Dapper?"

"That's his name. At least I think it is. You can clear that up when you meet with him."

I heard her tsk as she entered it on her keyboard.

"What's the problem exactly?"

"H-1 Visas. The feds seem to think he's bringing in Europeans with improper credentials."

"Any truth to that?"

"He says there's not."

"I'm sure. Is there an indictment?"

"No. Right now they're just swimming around, but you know how that goes."

"Yes, I do. Okay. What's the next step?"

"You may have to meet him in Crystal City. That's where he lives."

"I'm not a country doctor, Mr. Proctor."

"It's Joth, by the way. And yeah, me neither. Well, you see, he's a bit of a quirky guy. Guys with his kind of money often are."

Apparently, she heard the cash register ring.

"I might be able to make an exception if it's urgent."

"Can you meet him at, say, five-thirty on Friday?"

"Friday? Five-thirty? In Crystal City?"

"Look, this will be a high-profile case if it takes off. And Dapper pays for house calls."

That patched over the convenience problem, as I thought it would. Davison needed the business more than whatever she had planned for Friday evening. I gave her the contact information, including McNair's address.

"Okay. I'll call him."

"You might want to do that tomorrow. He just left here and his cell phone's down."

"Alright, thanks for the referral. I owe you one."

Referrals are the coin of the realm in my business. Just one can wash away a lot of doubts.

"I'll be looking for it."

I immediately dialed McNair. I got him on his cell, but it sounded like he wasn't home. Traffic whizzed by in the background as we exchanged a few pleasantries.

"You find me a lawyer yet?"

"As a matter of fact, that's why I'm calling. Emily Davison's her name. Check her out. She's with the Fuller firm, which is the name brand around here. Can you do this Friday at five-thirty?"

"Five-thirty in the afternoon? On Friday? Are you kidding?"

"Look, Dapper, it was hard for me to get her to fit you in."

"I can't. I'm heading up to Jersey."

"I'll tell you what. I'll get her to come to your place."

He hesitated.

"You'll like her. She's cute."

That did it.

"Okay, five-thirty on Friday at my place in Crystal City."

"I'll confirm it with her."

That left Jimmie. I had to find a way to get him out of his office on Friday afternoon.

Chapter Sixteen

Uncharted Waters

Heather called on Friday morning. I don't suppose anybody can get a call from the chief prosecutor on the day you're planning a crime and not be a little unnerved. However, this was worse than I feared.

"Is this your way of getting back at me?"

"I don't know what you're talking about, Heather."

"Leaving me hanging? When positions were reversed, I told you right away what I thought, and why."

I'd seen Heather legally exposed and professionally embarrassed, and vulnerable as a result, but she rarely lost her cool. This was something unexpected. She was talking about love.

"I don't know what I think. It's not that simple."

"You know whether you still love me."

I swallowed hard. Of course, it wasn't simple, but Heather saw things in black and white, truth and lies, right and wrong. She expected frankness to be immediately reciprocated.

"You're married to another man."

"Right now, I am."

"Right now?"

"You heard me."

"It's a lot of water under the bridge, Heather. I need some time."

She slammed down the phone without another word. My first reaction matched hers. I was about to call her back to re-engage and resolve this tiff before it could marinate, but I thought better of it and stopped myself. She had never done anything like this before, and it reminded me that the passage of years had taken us not only into uncharted waters, but into dangerous seas as well.

While Heather's call had unsettled me, the process of digesting it gave me an idea. I called Jimmie and reached him on his cell.

"The Commonwealth intends to serve a search warrant on you at your office on Friday afternoon."

He sounded as untroubled as if I had just told him he needed a haircut.

"Search warrant for what?"

"Evidence consistent with the maintenance of a gambling operation."

He laughed.

"Do they think I'm that stupid?"

"I don't think you want them nosing around."

"Where'd you get your information?"

"You've got your sources, and I've got mine."

"Like who?"

I was surprised at the name that popped into my head.

"Like Ish McGriff. Maybe you owe him one."

He ignored the comment. He might have had other sources in the courthouse, but probably no one he considered more reliable than me.

"Can you quash it?"

"Probably. I think I can talk Heather into withdrawing it, given a little time."

"What do you want me to do?"

"Make sure you're down at Irish Dan's having a beer Friday afternoon and don't come back. Get your secretary out of there, too. If no one's around, they can't serve the warrant. The sheriff will send it back marked 'no return.' Once it's public, I'll get a hold of it and tie 'em up over something."

"Thanks, that's very helpful."

"I doubt they'll even reissue it, once they realize you know it's coming."

Jimmie was always playing someone, including me. I had made my deal with the devil, but I had found a way to exact my pound of flesh in return. Battling Jimmie had become an end in itself.

"Great. I'll be in touch."

I was ready, or as ready as I would ever be. I assumed the same was true with DP.

Chapter Seventeen

The Jump

I was in the loading ramp of Jimmie's office building at 5:45 on Friday. It was a humid day, and under my green jumpsuit, my T-shirt was clinging to my back and my armpits were dripping sweat. Along with the jumpsuit, DP had given me a forest green baseball cap without a logo. I pulled the brim low over my eyes, ran my sweaty palms down the front of my suit and wondered if it was the right time to take up smoking.

I called up to the firm, asking for Grace Patrick, and was told that she was gone for the day. So far, so good. Emily Davison was known as a thorough and detailed attorney, so unless McNair took an immediate dislike to her, I figured we could bank on at least an hour of privacy if she came back at all, which was unlikely.

I felt shaky just the same. I told myself that this was nothing, that I had done worse, much worse, but I was unable to modulate the consuming guilt and self-loathing. At what point did I cross the line? At what point would I become a habitual criminal? Thus far, my sins had not caught up to me, but there was no guarantee that I would get away with this one.

I had pulled myself together by the time DP arrived, whistling a tune from *Mary Poppins* and pushing a laundry cart containing two backpack vacuum cleaners, several rolls of paper towels and a variety of industrial cleaning products. With his instinct for reading people, DP sized me up and squeezed my shoulder.

"If we don't do this right now, she'll be at his mercy."

"That's why I'm doing it. What about you?"

I'd asked DP that question a half dozen times in a myriad of different ways. He shrugged as if he'd never given it a moment's thought.

"I like a man who stands up for his friends."

That was as good an answer as any. We were in too deep to stop now. We exchanged grim nods and got immediately to work.

***

Access to the freight elevator was secure, but DP must have come by earlier in the day. The latch on the door was held back by a strip of silver duct tape and the door pushed open. Once I got the cart inside, I pulled off the tape and tossed it into the cart. DP pressed the button to summon the lift.

"So far so good."

We both pulled on surgical gloves and DP hopped nimbly into the cart.

"There's a security camera in the elevator," he said. "Keep your cap pulled low and your eyes on the floor. You'll be fine."

I nodded and covered him with the coarse, gray blanket he had placed in the cart for that purpose. The elevator doors opened and I rolled the cart inside. I punched the button for the top floor and the elevator lurched into life. The ride seemed interminable. I held my breath until the two-note electronic chime announced the sixth floor. As the doors opened with a wheeze, I sucked in my breath. DP's voice, muffled by the blanket, conveyed his usual calm.

"Just keep your head down and keep moving."

There was nothing else to do. I pushed open the glass doors to the firm's lobby and rolled the cart in, using a casual wave to keep a hand in front of my face. The receptionist was taking a call and her brow was knitted in concentration. She didn't even look up.

I knew the route from studying the floor plan so I didn't hesitate. I took an immediate left off the lobby and then another and continued down the broad, open corridor that reached the end of the office space. The firm was closing up for the weekend. Jokes and catcalls filled the air and I heard brief cases slamming shut. No one took note of the cleaning crew guy.

The offices of Davison and Patrick were set apart from the rest of the office by a large conference room. No one was inside and I ducked my head into both lawyer's offices. They were empty as well. Once inside Davison's office, I shut the door.

"All clear," I said.

DP didn't waste any time. He popped out of the cart and after sizing up the office and its furnishings, he made sure he had the boxcutter and flashlight and he hooked a stethoscope around his neck. I knew he'd use this to listen to the tumblers dropping inside the lock of Flambeau's safe. Moving with self-assured confidence, DP scampered to the top of a teak credenza and reached up with a mop handle to pop up the ceiling tile and slide it aside. I meshed my fingers together and gave him a boost. He put one hand on each side of the sustaining grid and up he went, like a squirrel scaling a tree. I got one of the backpack vacuums and swung my arms into the loops as DP replaced the tile into the grid. I was alone in the room. I looked at my watch. It was 6:10. The silence was unbearable.

I turned on the vacuum and sucked up the flakey white tile residue that DP had knocked loose. Then, I opened the door to the corridor and took a look: empty as a Sunday morning. I felt my heart rate slow down as I stepped fully into the role I had assumed. I vacuumed Davison's office, emptied her wastebasket and took my time doing it.

When I'd spent as much time in Davison's office as I thought prudent, I stepped next door and began vacuuming Patrick's space. Soon, I felt a tickle on my leg announcing a text vibrating into the phone in my pocket. I checked it. It was DP.

"I'm in."

Though I'd overcome my initial panic, the next few minutes seemed like a lifetime. I vacuumed, emptied waste baskets, dusted and polished until I worried that the spick and span state of the two women's offices on Monday morning might alert them that something wasn't quite right. Then my phone vibrated again.

"Coming back."

I went back into Davison's office and shut the door. A moment later, I heard what sounded like a raccoon in the ceiling. Then, the corner of the tile lifted from the grid and DP's dark eyes peered down.

"All clear?"

"Yes. Come on down."

He landed lightly on the balls of his feet on the top of the credenza. Then, he replaced the tile. He held up the flash drive and tossed it to me and I caught it. I also caught his expression, which was dour.

"Where's the Manet?"

"It wasn't there."

DP's energy and enthusiasm had piqued my interest in the Manet. I had what I wanted, but DP was so frustrated and impatient that I thought he might have another go at it.

"Did you look around?"

"Everywhere. You didn't say anything to him to tip him off?"

"Of course not."

With a dramatic sigh for his benefit, I again vacuumed the debris, then gestured to the cart. There was nothing else to do.

"Let's get out of here."

DP nodded. He calmly scanned the office for any uncovered tracks and then climbed back into the cart. I covered him with the blanket and looked at my watch. The whole thing had taken just under forty minutes. I checked to make sure that the flash drive was in my pocket and we left.

Back in the lobby, I pushed the button to summon the freight elevator. When it arrived, the doors opened to reveal the real cleaning crew. There were two men and a woman dressed in similar green jump suits, but each one had the corporate logo on the left breast. I tipped my cap and stepped back to allow them to exit the elevator car. Then, I stepped in and pushed "B1." The doors closed before the real crew had a chance to react.

The doors opened on B1 and DP climbed out of the cart. We both peeled off our jumpsuits. We tossed them in the cart and covered them with the blanket. Once out on the street, we rolled down Wilson Boulevard like two proud parents with a baby carriage. I broke the silence.

"What happened to the Manet?"

"I was gonna ask you that."

"It was on the wall last time I was there."

DP shook his head.

"It's a mystery."

Yes, another mystery.

But Heather was no longer at the mercy of Jimmie Flambeau, and I felt a rare sense of exhilaration.

Chapter Eighteen

The Spoils of the Crime

I gave DP a few minutes to complete a task I wanted
no part of: inspecting the flash drive. When I rejoined
him upstairs, he scrunched up his face and nodded.

"That's it, Joth. It's a video of Heather's husband and
Crandall. It's got to be the one you got at the Pelham."

The Major Pelham was a rural inn owned and operated by Bobbitt Justice, a former client of mine. That's
where Justice had captured the sexually explicit video of
Peter Peacock with Heather's top deputy. It was also
where Jimmie Flambeau mangled Bobbitt's fingers to
force her to turn the flash drive over to him.

I'd had it in my hands that day, but I gave it to Jimmie, who snookered me with a blank when I asked him
to return it. I had no regrets for what I had just done.
Instead of guilt, I felt the same surge of elation that
probably creates career criminals.

I had beaten Jimmie, and I had gotten away with it—
at least so far.

DP destroyed the flash drive with a hammer. I'd expected this scene to bring closure for me, but there were still too many loose ends for that.

"Victory at last," I said. "How long you think until Jimmie notices it's gone?"

"Not until he tries to use it."

"He's not going to be happy."

"He'll be humiliated. A guy in Jimmie's profession can't afford to look like a fool."

I had just committed a crime but I felt as clean as a repentant sinner.

"Can I buy you a drink?"

DP flashed his crooked smile but shook his head. He was in no mood to celebrate.

"I've got work to do."

The discouragement was all over his round face. He had wanted that Manet, and I knew there was nothing I could say to ease his disappointment.

***

I waited until the next week when the calendar changed, assuming, rightly as it turned out, that both Ish and Mitch would promptly get me October's rent. Mitch came in to my office, whimpering, and promised repeatedly that he'd never be late again. Ish provided a healthy chunk toward the arrears.

It was just after two when I packed the stacks of bills into two separate envelopes, put them in my briefcase, and headed over to Flambeau's. Helen admitted me as if I'd been expected. I knew my battle with Jimmie wasn't over, but taking a lead into the fourth quarter provoked a warm sensation.

I took my usual seat and snuck a quick glance at the safe while Jimmie counted the cash with his usual precision. Nothing looked out of place, but there was no sign of the Manet.

Jimmie straightened the stacks of bills.

"I like a man who knows the value of cash, Joth. That was something I could never get through Felipe's thick head."

He wrapped each stack with a thick rubber band, marked each with the debtor's name and booked the payments on his ledger. Then, he put the ledger back in a drawer, locked it, and settled back in his chair.

He smiled at me.

"I'm usually right about people and I was right about you. We're going to do a lot of good work together."

"You get rich, Jimmie. What do I get?"

This was a topic that appealed to Flambeau: horse trading, looking for an edge, matching wits. I was sure he viewed me as unprepared for the street games he excelled at, and I wanted to keep it that way. I was also worried he might be right.

"You expecting a little bonus?"

"Nope. I just did my job. You don't get a bonus for that where I come from."

"Fair enough. But you did good work efficiently. And you got wind of that search warrant and you shut it down. That's extra. That should be rewarded."

"Okay. I'm not one to look a gift horse in the mouth."

"What do you have in mind?"

I allowed myself a few moments, giving the impression of careful consideration.

"My father dealt in cash, too, but he saw the advantage in picking up tangible items when he could. What happened to that little painting that was here last week?"

"You think what you did is worth three thousand four hundred dollars?"

"Don't you?"

Jimmie narrowed his eyes and studied me. He liked a man who pushed back, and that's why I did it. At least that was part of the reason. His appraisal of me had probably just jumped several notches.

"In lieu of fees?"

147

"I thought we were talking about a bonus."

He laughed.

"Well, it doesn't matter, does it? The guy took it back."

"Took it back? He doesn't sound like the kind of guy you should be playing cards with."

"No, he's perfect. Not a pigeon, but a guy I can handle."

I knew Jimmie felt that way about me, and that was okay, as long as it wasn't true.

He studied the safe, and for a moment I thought he might have spotted something out of place, some clue that someone had been in there, but I was just anxious. Recognizing this, I dialed it back and waited for Jimmie to continue.

"Stuff like that painting, more often than not it's just collateral. Guy wants to stay in the game and he's short of cash, so he puts up something of value. We were playing at his place. Nothing to it."

"So, it was a stake holder. Literally."

"Exactly. He came in Friday morning with the cash."

"How'd you know it was worth the stake?"

"To tell you the truth, I didn't, but I had him hooked and I didn't want to let him get away."

"I don't play cards, Jimmie, but if I did, I think I'd go into the game knowing exactly how much I was willing to lose."

"That's why I like playing cards with McNair. He doesn't think that way."

I swallowed and hoped Jimmie didn't notice.

"McNair?"

"Yeah. Dapper McNair. He claims to be some kind of art expert. You know the kind. Pretentious."

"Local guy?"

"No, a guy from up your way."

He turned up his hands.

"He knows a lot of the same people I know, so it wasn't really much of a risk."

"Sure."

I got up.

"Well, you don't owe me anything else Jimmie. Just keep me in mind at Christmas."

***

Back at the office, I put a call in to Emily Davison. When she picked up, I had to remind her that I'd sent her a potential client.

"Oh yeah, McNair. That didn't go well."

"Mind if I ask why?"

"Yeah. He doesn't like women."

That sounded right, but I made excuses for him.

"His business revolves around women."

"Maybe he doesn't like it when a woman tells him what he doesn't want to hear."

"You mean, like writing you a check?"

"No, I mean like listening to my advice."

As far as I knew, McNair didn't yet have a problem and I didn't think Davison would give him more than a general outline of her views and what she could do for him at an initial meeting. That shouldn't have provided much to quarrel about.

"I'm sorry to put you to all that trouble for something that didn't pan out."

"Don't worry about it. You have to kiss a lot of frogs in this business."

Yes, you do. Especially if you're self-employed.

Chapter Nineteen

Imagine a Couple of Jamokes

Although I found Jimmie Flambeau repulsive, I enjoyed the battle of wills and wits that was at the heart of our relationship, not because I usually won these little face-offs, but because I relished mixing it up with him. And there was value in these encounters. I always came away from his office with a new challenge or a clarification of an old one.

The unexpected connection between McNair and Flambeau sounded like a little of both, so I called McNair.

"You work it out with Davison?"

"As a matter of fact, we didn't."

The tone in his voice was flip and indignant.

"Something wrong?"

"You mean other than she's a bitch?"

"You mean you can't push her around? Isn't that the kind of lawyer you want?"

"You consider her cute?"

"I didn't think that would be important to you."

"Alright, I'm a chauvinist pig. I admit it. Why can't you do this yourself?"

"I already explained that to you, Dapper. I don't want to create a conflict that would keep me from representing Irish Dan."

"Nothing's going to happen with Irish Dan."

"Plus the fact that I'm not an immigration lawyer."

"The feds are just poking around. Sooner or later, they're going to realize there's nothing to look at. I just want you to expedite that process."

He waited, assessing the persuasiveness of this line. I didn't encourage him. When I didn't respond, he picked up the thread again.

"I need a fixer. Dan says that's what you do."

"That's not going to happen, Dapper. I'm happy to find you someone else."

He paused, as if he were considering the wisdom of turning to something else.

"There are other items, Joth. Maybe bigger, more important things. We need to talk. Can you come by? It's on the clock."

It was the middle of the week, and I had nothing to do.

"No commitment. Got it? But I'll listen to what you have to say."

"That's all I'm asking."

***

Driving to Crystal City, I reflected on McNair's words and his manner of speaking. Something didn't fit. For one thing, he acted pestered about this U.S. Attorney probe, but he hadn't asked for a referral to another lawyer. Instead, he wanted me to do something I wasn't qualified to do.

McNair was simultaneously brusque and oily. He rubbed me the wrong way, but he also piqued my curiosity, like a Rubik's Cube. He had convinced me that he was gaming someone or something, and that was closer to my line of work.

I slid into a spot in a surface lot near Dan's place. The afternoon was seasonably chilly, with a stiff breeze, and I used the short walk up 23rd Street and into the adjacent neighborhood to sift through the possibilities. Nothing made complete sense, so I decided to take it as it came.

McNair seemed to be waiting for me. He escorted me back to the sitting room where we'd met on my previous visit. He moved slowly, like a man with a heavy cold, and the effort seemed to tire him. He sat, and after gathering his breath, he asked me if I wanted anything to drink. I didn't, but what I saw in that room made me say yes. It was the Manet I'd last seen hanging above Jimmie Flambeau's safe.

"Whiskey alright?"

"Rum if you have it."

"Sure. You take it with Coke?"

"Unless you want to make me a daiquiri."

I did not expect him to take this request seriously, but he did; or at least he acted upon it.

After McNair stepped into the kitchen, I got out of my chair and took a careful look at the painting, now hanging at eye level on the wall beside the fireplace. It seemed identical to the one I'd seen in Jimmie's office, right down to the simple metal frame. When I heard the whirr of a blender, I calculated that I had time for a closer inspection so I stepped forward, studying it from every angle, estimating the size, considering the brushstrokes and comparing it to my recollection of the painting Jimmie said was plunder from a poker game. I didn't know if I was looking at loot from the Gardner heist, but I was ready to bet that this painting, and the one I'd seen in Jimmie's office, were one and the same.

"Seen that before?"

McNair had quietly re-entered the room and was now standing behind me, a sly smile on his face and a cocktail glass in each hand.

"A friend of mine won something like this in a card game not too long ago."

He handed me my drink and dropped painfully into an armchair. Once settled, he let an expression of smug satisfaction blossom on his face. It was the look of someone who holds all the cards, or at least thinks he does.

"If Jimmie Flambeau told you that, he's lying."

As I sat down in the cushioned armchair facing the painting, something clicked. A sudden surge like a rogue wave broke over me, and I now understood the source of Flambeau's otherwise inexplicable knowledge of my father and his gambling habits. My mind began to race, as if I were still a boy under my father's spell. I focused on staying in the moment.

"That's not quite what he said, Dapper. He told me he'd taken it as security on a bet for some guy who couldn't cover the ante."

McNair uncrossed his legs and took a long pull at his drink. In the bright light of the room, the skin on his face had an unhealthy yellow tone. This was a worn-out man. But he was still insistent and sure of his opinions. He was a man who made little effort to smooth his rough edges.

He cleared his throat.

"Flambeau's a hell of a card player."

"He cheats, you know."

McNair laughed, as if cheating was part of the entertainment.

"Everybody cheats. He's good at it."

"So, how come you stayed in the game?"

He snickered, as if he'd lost a round he could afford to lose.

"I don't think I'll invite him back."

"Too good for you?"

The barb stuck.

"He didn't even know what it was."

"You wouldn't have put it up if he did, right?"

He took another drink.

"But you do."

"Yeah, I do."

"Then, you no doubt recognize that."

He pointed to the landscape painting over the mantlepiece, the one I had noticed on my first visit to his place—the one portraying an eerie autumn landscape built around an obelisk. I hadn't then, but following this clue, I thought through the inventory of Gardner loot DP had pulled up on his computer. I now recognized that this painting was among the stolen items that DP had scrolled through. If McNair was telling the truth, the paintings above his mantlepiece, and on the wall beside it, were not just part of art history; they were part of American folklore.

"Sure. I saw that when it hung in the Gardner, too."

McNair chuckled and nodded.

"You must have been a kid then."

"Yeah, I was."

"Your father take you?"

"As a matter of fact, he did."

"Ancient history."

He rested his chin on his hand, looked at me, and mused.

"Imagine Joth, just imagine. A couple of jamokes from the opposite sides of Boston. They stroll into the Isabella Stewart Gardner one night and come out an hour and a half later with five hundred million dollars worth of art. Five hundred million! It's one of the greatest, boldest acts in human history."

He evaluated my reaction before continuing, and he leaned forward to make his next point.

"I planned the heist and pulled it off without a hitch and now, today, nobody knows nothing about it."

"Correction. A lot of people know something about it."

"Well, that's true. But I get no credit for it and maybe never will."

"Isn't that the price you pay if you do the job right?"

"But there should be some payoff."

He took a sip of his daiquiri.

"Then, why did you do it?"

He sat back and sighed. The wig and the evidence of illness on his face made it hard to pinpoint Dapper's age, but he was getting older fast. He was happy to disappear into the glories of his youth, whether real or imagined.

"I saw the opportunity. We took the art off the wall and disappeared into the night. Voila. And the loot? Who knows what happened to the loot?"

We?

I focused on that word. Who else made up this *we*?

McNair shook his head and drank deeply.

"Somebody might remember the Vermeer, but the rest of it? Just vague memories from an art class. But the Vermeer . . ."

He drank again and sighed.

"The Vermeer?"

"*The Concert*, Joth. Painted by a Dutchman named Johannes Vermeer in the 1600s. Now, I know you heard about that, right, and don't say you didn't. The most valuable painting stolen from the Gardner. By far."

I came up with some light laughter.

"That's not something you can throw in the pot in a friendly poker game and expect no one to notice."

I expected him to laugh, but he didn't seem to hear me. Instead, he sighed wistfully.

"Last time I checked, the reward for the Vermeer was ten million dollars. Just for the Vermeer."

"Are you in the habit of checking?"

He looked up.

"No. Why should I? I don't have the Vermeer."

I'd been treading carefully. I saw that he expected me to have some knowledge of this subject and he was probing the edges of it.

"But you've got two others. The Manet and this land-scape."

He got up painfully and walked up to the painting over the fireplace.

"You know what? In 1990, everyone said this paint-ing was by Rembrandt. Now the so-called experts say it was painted by his pupil. Some fucker named Flinck. You know why they say that?"

"Because it's true?"

He flicked an index finger against it.

"This is a fucking Rembrandt! They don't want no-body selling it for what it's worth. That's why."

"Are you planning on selling it?"

He sneered and sat down again.

"Okay, wise guy. Now let's talk about what you got. Or what you can get."

He had approached this subject slowly enough that I'd been able to process it and follow the thread of where he was going. I put the question of his veracity out of my mind for the moment and summoned a confidential chuckle.

"I'm not ready to talk to you about that, Dapper."

"You need another drink?"

I held up my half-full glass. He went into the kitchen to pour what remained in the blender into his.

What you can get?

I saw now what he was hinting at and fought the instinct to overreact. Was McNair suggesting that my father had ended up holding some of the loot from the Gardner job? It wasn't impossible. My dad was no jamoke, but he was a gambler. He was also a man widely known as an honest broker. John Proctor would have been a logical choice as a sort of short-term escrow agent while Dapper addressed the many unanticipated consequences of his crime.

I put my drink down beside me on the floor. Like my dad, I knew the dangers of alcohol.

When Dapper returned, I didn't wait for him to sit down.

"Where's the rest of it?"

He tilted his head to peer at me. This was what he was waiting for: real talk, man to man, or at least as he saw it.

"I was hoping you could help me with some of that."

"That's what I figured."

"And?"

"What's in it for me?"

"It depends on what you've got. Or can get your hands on."

"That makes sense."

"Come on, Proctor. I put my cards on the table."

"I'm just a careful guy."

"Like your dad."

I still couldn't understand how my dad figured into this tale and his inclusion made me wary of Dapper's entire tale.

"If you knew my father, you knew he was."

"Why do you think I picked him? I'll tell you why. It was because he was an outsider. He could fly under the radar."

I wet my lips.

"And you?"

"I masterminded the whole thing. From soup to nuts. The idea was mine. And nobody knows it."

At this stage of his life, was the renown he would gain more valuable to him than any financial recovery? It sounded like it.

"When was the last time you talked to my dad?"

Dapper took a labored breath and seemed to be hunting back in his mind.

"I'm not sure I've talked to him in this century. So, maybe he's dead, too. If so, I'm truly sorry. But that means only you know where it is."

It?

He closed an eye and looked at me shrewdly, then took another long pull at his drink. He was no longer being careful.

"The heist, yeah, I should get credit for that. But there were things I didn't think about. The big problem? See, back then, all big crime in Boston got cleared by certain people. I didn't do that. I didn't even know that's how it worked. When they found out, well, let's just say, it wasn't okay."

"So, there was pressure, and not just from the police?"

"Oh yeah. There was pressure. They wanted their piece."

"Did you give it to them?"

He slumped in the chair and a distant expression came over his eyes.

"It was crazy. I was dodging everybody: the cops, the bosses. And then I told the bosses what we had, but it didn't match up with what the museum reported as stolen. That's where the real trouble started."

"But it didn't really matter, did it? No one could sell any of it any way."

"It took everyone a while to figure that out, too."

I was piecing it all together, trying to parlay my limited knowledge while staying one step ahead of him. And, on top of that, there was the matter of my father.

"So, what's different about now?"

"The statute of limitations is what's different. No one can be prosecuted for the robbery now. That ship has sailed."

I knew the statute of limitation for grand larceny in Massachusetts was six years.

"The statute expired years ago."

"Yeah. And all that time, I've been staring at three concrete walls and a row of steel bars in Walpole. That's how they got back at me. They set me up for an armored car robbery that I had no part in. And every day I woke up in that hell hole, I imagined the day I'd cash in. Now, they're all dead, the guys who set me up. All of 'em gone."

"But the stuff's still hot worldwide. You can't sell any of it. Not if you want anything close to real value."

McNair gave me a thin smile and tilted his head. And then, the last piece fell into place.

"But someone can claim the reward," I said.

"Are you familiar with the reward?"

"Just what you told me. Ten million for everything. But we don't have everything."

"We got enough. We got enough to make them open their wallet. If you've got what I think you've got, the sky's the limit."

"I'm not committing to anything yet."

Dapper summoned up an angry glare, but the effort seemed to cause him physical pain.

"Listen to me, Joth. Everything's worth more as part of a big package. Even the Vermeer."

I studied this aging crook and con man. He was bald under that wig. The jaundiced face and a sometimes wheezy and breathless manner suggested a person in constant pain. Cancer? I wondered. He was desperate to bring this multi-decade chase to a conclusion. On top of that, he seemed exhausted. He'd have less and less fight within him with each passing day and he understood that.

I thought about his point. Despite its remaining trove of irreplaceable art, the Gardner was a small local museum and the heist had been an enormous hit. Not only was its collection diminished, so was its prestige. For a few years after, curious visitors had bolstered ticket sales with the lurid enthusiasm of rubberneckers at a fatal accident, but as the immediacy of the robbery faded, attendance languished. Recovery of any of the items would be a shot in the arm and I guessed that the Gardner would be willing to pay top dollar to reacquire it.

"And that's why you need me?"

"That's part of it. I'm on their radar. I've been on their radar since it happened. You? You're a prominent lawyer six states away."

"How's this going to work?"

His eyes glistened.

"You can meet with the Gardner. Big press conference. You tell 'em exactly how I did it. I'll give you all the details. You negotiate the reward, and we can divvy it up."

"Divvy it up how?"

"I've got two items. The Manet and the landscape. I know you got the finial, but that's the least valuable thing in the lot. So, unless you've got more than the finial, I figure eighty percent of the reward you negotiate goes to me. If you've got something bigger, those numbers can change."

The finial.

I remembered it. He was referring to the imperial eagle figurehead that sat atop a French battle standard from the Napoleonic wars. It was the oddest and most eccentric of the items taken.

"There's one more thing, Dapper. My fee for the negotiation."

He dropped his eyes.

"Yeah, we can cut that in."

He leaned forward, kneading his stubby fingers between his knees. He had waited decades for this day.

"I've got reason to believe that your dad has more than just the finial."

There it was: my dad.

"Maybe."

"Can you imagine how thrilled they're going to be to get anything back after all these years? We're talking a lot of money here. And no one goes to jail."

McNair's growing excitement was overcoming his prudence. He was speaking like a starving man.

"Okay. I can handle it."

"I want to see the goods first."

"That'll take some time. They're not in Virginia."

"They?"

"If you really know my dad, you would know that."

"Where are they?"

His response sounded a little too anxious and I made sure he knew I'd heard it. I chuckled.

"I'll let you know when I've got everything in hand. Now, about my fee. I'll take ten percent off the top."

He shook his head sadly.

"I don't think so. This is lawyer's work. I'll pay you a lawyer's fee."

"A percentage is customary in a case like this."

"There is no case like this! You bill your time at five hundred dollars an hour. That'll come off the top."

"I don't think that'll work."

Shaking my head sadly, I stood up to leave. Dapper was out of his chair as quickly as his tired body would permit. He stepped toward me and put a sweaty palm on my chest.

"Hang on."

"What's the rush?"

He dropped his hand and took a step back.

"You don't know what you're doing, Proctor. We've hung on to this stuff too long already. You understand that?"

I did. The Manet and the Flinck were two unique and valuable items, but they could be stolen from him with impunity. Now that I knew he had them, he was increasingly at risk every day they remained in his possession.

"You've been hanging on to them for years."

"I can put 'em back on ice, but I don't want that. I want to move now."

"My fee is ten percent of the total."

"Five percent against my two objects. No commission on the finial."

"I'll see you around, Dapper."

His voice and eyes dropped.

"Ten percent. No commission on the finial. Anything else you have, we'll talk."

I stuck out my hand and he shook it. I didn't trust him as far as I could throw him, which was probably across the room, but once I had the Manet and the Flinck, I didn't need to worry about trusting him.

"Let me make some calls. I'll be in touch."

***

I held it together until I made it back to my car. With my hands on the wheel, I broke into a cold sweat and began to shake. The Dutch Fucker was one thing. Johannes Vermeer was the creator of an exquisite oil painting, called *The Concert*. It was the crown jewel of the Gardner theft, even more valuable than the Rembrandts. Dapper McNair, the man who'd hit the Gardner, believed my father had it.

Dapper had taken me on a sick ride back to my youth. It took me more than ten minutes before I was able to drive out of the lot.

Chapter Twenty

A Journey Through the Mists of Time

I took the stairs up to DP's lair. The door was open. Behind his desk, I could see his pale visage in the reflection on the PC's monitor. I turned on the overhead light to announce myself and shut the door. He swiveled around and measured my expression.

"This looks important."

"It might be."

I paced around the room with my hands shoved deeply into my pockets.

"I've got something for you. It might be an opportunity. It might be a risk."

He shrugged calmly.

"Either way."

I recounted my meeting with McNair, sparing no detail. DP listened with growing interest. When I finished, he swiveled away and stared out the window.

"That's why he wanted to see you?"

"What do you mean?"

"I mean the immigration thing. That was just a ruse?"

"I don't think so."

"Think again, my friend. You hooked him up with a top immigration lawyer, just like he asked, and he rejected her flat. He didn't even ask for another referral. Think about it. What he really wanted was a credible introduction to you and he got one from Dan."

"He went to a lot of trouble. The girls from eastern Europe."

"Wake up. One of them plays the piano. So what? He probably picked up a pair of bleached blondes from south Jersey and taught them to spout a few lines of gibberish that sound eastern European. He got 'em a pretty good gig."

"You're right. As usual. But why?"

DP winked and I followed his train of thought.

"I think you found out today, Joth."

Then I came to what was really troubling me.

"McNair seems to think that my dad has some of the Gardner loot."

"How?"

"I think he asked my dad to hold some of it. Right after the robbery."

As I spoke the words out loud for the first time, I felt their weight and sat down heavily. DP gave me some time.

"Is that possible?"

"McNair did the Gardner job. He admitted that to me today. He and another guy. My dad was a gambler. People knew who he was and he was known as a dependable guy. McNair was an amateur. He didn't know you needed the okay of the crime bosses before pulling off something like the Gardner. When they found out about it, they demanded their piece. He was getting squeezed from both sides. So, he parked some of the stuff with my father."

"He told you that?"

"Yeah."

"What stuff?"

I hesitated, not because I didn't trust DP, but because I didn't trust my own understanding. I didn't know my father's exact role, or if he had even played one. I thought back to the cold day when my father had dragged me unwillingly to visit an eccentric museum which housed what I would later learn was a world class collection of art.

When was it that we were there? I tried to remember the weather and what grade I would have been in.

"I don't know. It's hard for me to believe it even happened, But some of what McNair said rings too true."

"He must have told you something about it."

"Well, for one thing, he thinks my dad has the finial that was on top of the Napoleonic battle standard."

171

"A bronze imperial eagle."

"That's right."

He had the Gardner website up and had paged down to the finial.

"Joth, the reward for the finial is $100,000. Dapper McNair didn't go to all this trouble to get his hands on something worth $100,000."

"Yeah. He thinks I've got something else. Or that my dad does."

"What's that?"

I couldn't believe I was about to say it out loud.

"The Vermeer."

"*The Concert*?"

I nodded.

DP dropped his head onto his arms and folded them across the top of his desk. Finally, he looked up.

"What about your dad? Are you going to ask him?"

"Not unless you can find him."

DP's thin eyebrows arched up.

"My father abandoned the family."

"When was that?"

"Well, it was after the Gardner."

DP nodded gravely.

"Have you heard from him since?"

"No. I'm pretty sure my mother did, but she wouldn't talk about it. I'm pretty sure he sent her money periodically."

"Why do you think he left?"

"They hadn't been getting along for years."

"You could ask her about it."

"She died years ago."

"I see."

DP got up and went slowly to the window. I understood that the pause was intended as a tactful way to introduce a new subject. I appreciated his concern, but the heavy silence only reinforced my sense of being rowed out to sea by some unseen force.

"What do we know about McNair?"

"Not much. There were a lot of suspects in the heist. They've all been run down. I never heard McNair's name mentioned."

"Is that why they never found the paintings? They never identified the real criminals?"

DP went back behind his computer and the website he'd pulled up.

"I wonder what McNair's real name is."

I didn't reply.

"Hey. Take a look at this."

On the day after the robbery, a police artist had interviewed the two guards and had created sketches of the two faux cops who had pulled it off. I had never seen them before and stared in disbelief at DP's computer screen.

"What do you think?"

I thought one of them looked like a much younger version of the man I knew as Dapper McNair. But that wasn't what took my breath away.

I sat down. Then, I tapped the screen.

"DP, that looks like my dad."

It was a rare circumstance that could shock DP Tran.

"Are you sure?"

"Of course not. It's a sketch."

"Right. It's just a sketch. Thousands of people look like that."

"Yeah, I suppose."

"So, where is he, Joth? And how are we going to find out?"

I shook my head, then walked to the window and took a breath. The guilt and exhilaration I'd experienced in pulling off the caper with DP in Jimmie Flambeau's office had unsettled me. I lacked the confidence in my own judgment that would be necessary to reach any clear-eyed conclusions about the Gardner mystery, and the possibility that my own father might have been involved left me even further at sea. But I wasn't going to walk away from it.

"I don't know what to think about all of this. I just know that McNair thinks I can get my hands on at least one of the hottest objects in the art world. If that's what he thinks, I'm willing to let him."

"What's next?"

"He wants me to negotiate the return of the stuff to the Gardner."

"Are you gonna do it?"

"Of course. I might find my father."

Chapter Twenty-One

Back to Work

My father had always been a mystery to me, even when we were living in the same house. He had a way of talking in riddles and hypotheticals, as if he were afraid of giving a secret away through any uninhibited exchange of ideas. Was this strange old man from my native state really offering to crack open a long-closed door for me?

All of this was too much for one day. Too much to process, too much personal baggage to weigh. I needed to put those questions aside until they began to make sense.

Something happened the next morning that helped. Marie announced a client: Father John Tedesco. This was just what I needed— something to occupy my mind, for a few minutes, at least.

"Show him in."

In Virginia, a grand jury witness is entitled to attend the hearing accompanied by counsel, but the lawyer cannot participate. Although seen-but-not-heard, an experienced lawyer making his presence known and making sure procedures are adhered to tends to act as an informal restraint on a prosecutor who might run a little far afield. In addition to keeping the prosecutor honest, the presence of a lawyer tends to stiffen the backbone of the witness.

Nothing was going to stiffen John Tedesco's backbone, but what I had on Sue Crandall had made me feel confident enough to allow John to go in naked, as they say. There was always a risk involved in that choice, particularly without a grant of immunity, but there were larger issues for Father John, and I thought this gesture would send the right message to his congregation without exposing him to any legal jeopardy.

And I was right for a change.

He stepped into my office looking light on his feet in a pair of spiffy new Allbirds, smiling like a man whose conscience feels as light as his feet. Before he sat down, he pulled a wad of bills from the inside pocket of his gray flannel sport coat. He sat down and started counting through his stash of tens and twenties.

"I've got half of it, Joth. I'll give you the other half next week."

I raised an open palm.

"Keep it. Add it to Sunday's collection."

I didn't trust priests who dealt in cash. In fact, I didn't trust anyone who dealt in cash. And I knew I needed a friend in heaven more than I needed the money.

"Thanks, I will."

"All of it, John."

He blushed and slid the money carefully back into his jacket pocket.

"I assume it went well? The grand jury."

He chuckled, a man at ease.

"It went very well. She had a script and she stuck to it."

"Did she ask about anything beyond the letter?"

"Nope. She just wanted to find out what Pasquale wanted and what I did."

What she wanted from John was for the grand jury to learn that Pasquale had taken steps consistent with what a rather dense murderer might do to cover his crime. He ran through it for me, and it was both what I hoped for and what I expected. The bulk of the testimony Crandall needed, the nuts and the bolts, would have come from the coroner, the investigating officer, and others with facts to contribute. Crandall was good. She knew how to put the case together in a simple, tight and streamlined manner, and a man in a Roman collar nodding his head at every question she asked could only help.

"I assume she'll get an indictment. I'll call you when I hear something."

"Thanks, Joth."

But his brow furrowed, and he didn't get up.

"There is one other thing I'd like to talk to you about."

I sighed. This could be a lot of things, none of them good.

"It's about Melanie."

I didn't expect that, and the sound of her name raised my blood pressure for an uncomfortable moment.

"What about her?"

A lot of people shrank back a bit when I responded in that gruff tone, but not Father John. He recognized a paper tiger when he heard one growl. He smiled.

"Well, to be frank Joth, I don't think you're treating her right."

"What business is that of yours?"

It was a dumb thing to say. Melanie was alone in the world, and she'd put her trust in her priest. He was now fearless in standing up for her.

"She's a woman who forms strong attachments. Don't let her get attached to you, Joth. Unless she's in your long-term plans."

Melanie Freeman was a person of uncomplicated decency, and I don't run into too many like that. She was also sexy as hell, but I had too much baggage at the moment to carry any more. It was time to come clean.

"I don't have any long-term plans."

"Well, she does. Or she'd like to. Have you talked to her about that?"

"What did she tell you?"

"I don't want you to think that she's asked me to interfere. Or that she's complained to me. I see her every day and she's not a hard person to read."

I had dated John's sister and he probably assumed I had been sleeping with her, but that relationship hadn't generated this sort of scrutiny. That was because John knew that I had loved his sister. That was the difference. It was also his point.

"Treat her right, Joth. She deserves it."

He got up and when he shook my hand, he looked at me as if he'd just assigned me my penance.

I had always known this day was inevitable. Melanie wasn't the woman for me, and John knew this better than I did. I couldn't put my finger on the reason. I liked, even admired Melanie, but the attraction was purely physical. She saw me as a project, a soul to be redeemed. Our contact points had never formed a connected circuit. But he was right. It wasn't fair to continue a relationship that would never develop beyond the superficial.

I was still thinking this over when I got a call from Sue Crandall. She sounded friendly and obsequious, calling me "Mr. Proctor," which was odd, since we'd been on a first-name basis for several years.

"The grand jury brought back an indictment today against Felipe Pasquale. Second degree murder."

"Second degree?"

"Well, we really don't know what was going on in his head that day, do we?"

I had to give her credit. There were no eyewitnesses, and the case was entirely circumstantial. It was a very good result.

"There's not much in that guy's head, but it's all evil."

"I've heard he left town. If he shows up again, he won't be on the street for long."

I thanked her for the effort and thought about calling Heather. Congratulations was in order. This would be a load off her mind and would improve her reelection prospects. But I thought better of it. Instead, I called Melanie.

Melanie could be chatty, and she was today. I let her run on until I sensed an opening.

"We need to talk."

She paused as she absorbed the subtext.

"Yes, I suppose we do."

"Is now a good time? A cup of coffee, maybe?"

"I'm on the Mall. We could meet down here."

"What mall?"

I assumed she meant a shopping center.

"The National Mall."

"Oh. Okay. Where are you?"

"The National Gallery. There's a café downstairs."

"I'll be there in half an hour."

I knew where the National Gallery was located but I had no idea where to park. Consequently, I was half an hour late. Melanie prized punctuality as a cardinal virtue, so I expected her to be steaming. She wasn't. The only thing steaming was a cup of tea she was stirring with a mechanical repetitiveness, her chin propped in her other hand.

"Sorry I'm late. Parking."

"The parking's terrible. You must be new to D.C."

I sat down heavily and decided against coffee. I didn't want to prolong the interview and neither did she.

The National Gallery's café is built into the subterranean bridge space that joins the east and west buildings of the museum. The only natural light comes through a cascading waterfall built behind a glass wall about fifty yards from where we were sitting. It was mid-afternoon and most of the tables were empty.

"You spend a lot of time here?"

It was an obvious conversation starter, the sort of comment that could be ignored or might solicit a similarly banal response in most circumstances.

"You don't have any idea where I spend my time, do you?"

"You know, Melanie, this isn't going like I thought it would."

"How did you think it would go?"

I sighed. She was not going to make it easy.

"I don't know."

"That says all that needs to be said, doesn't it?"

"I suppose it does."

She stood up and reached out to shake my hand. I stood up as I took it.

"Thanks for some good times, Joth."

"Yes, we had some good times."

With that, she walked with great dignity toward the escalator, and I watched her go, a slender, poised and lonely woman leaving behind a lonely man. I told myself it should have worked. It could have worked, but that was not true. There was no magic between us and there never would be, and I was sorry about that.

I gave it a few minutes and went upstairs to the main gallery, where I asked a daydreaming security guard for directions to the French Impressionists. He pointed out the way, and I found a work by Edouard Manet in a west building gallery, a painting of a pale woman with Gallic features seated in front of a wrought iron fence. The woman eyes the painter with an ambiguous expression, while beside her, a child peers through the fence at a gray cloud of locomotive smoke, the herald of changing times.

The painting is called *The Railway*, and I thought I could recognize stylistic similarities with *Chez Tortoni*, such as the direct gaze and detachment of the subject, the use of subdued colors, and what looked like impulsive freedom in the brush strokers. But strolling through the same gallery, I came upon works by another French Impressionist, named Monet, who was not the same guy, although as far as I could tell, the fluid and subtle brush strokes might have been the work of the same painter.

Asking me to distinguish between Edouard Manet and Claude Monet was like asking me to judge horse-flesh just because it was something my father could do. You needed an art expert to tell whether the *Chez Tortoni* I had first seen in Flambeau's office and then in McNair's place was the genuine item. I'd just have to take it on faith. Or maybe the whole thing McNair had cooked up was an elaborate scam leading to a payoff I couldn't fathom.

Chapter Twenty-Two

The Last Day of Winter

It was four o'clock when I got back to the office, and I was drained from two long days. When that mood hit, I was in the habit of taking a walk across Wilson Boulevard to Ireland's Four Courts, where I could have a drink and chat up Phyliss, the pretty bartender who works the happy hour shift. Instead, I let my better angels rule me and walked up to DP's office. I knocked on his door jam. When he looked up, he recognized my expression.

"I was just thinking of you, Joth."

"Yeah?"

I sat down across from his desk.

"What is it today?"

"I just broke up with my girlfriend. Among other things."

"Other things?"

"I think you know."

"Dapper McNair?"

"I don't know what he's up to, or why he's dragging my dad and me into all this."

DP put his chin in his hand.

"He gave you a lot to think about."

"He did."

"Did you make any progress?"

"Not really. I thought Dan had brought me a case. But it's more than that, DP. This is my life. McNair's called up a lot of hazy memories and I can't figure out how to put them together."

He let that thought sit before he spoke.

"I might be able to help you with that."

"I was hoping you could."

He pointed to the overstuffed lounge chair in the far corner of the room.

"Let's get more comfortable."

I did as he suggested, disappearing into its cracked red leather, reclining the back and raising the leg rest. He pulled the window shades, turned down the lights and threw a light-weight blanket over my legs. I pulled it gratefully up to my chin. I hadn't felt the stress build through the day, but now I felt it recede.

"Empty your head, Joth. We'll just talk a little."

I shut my eyes. That part was easy. Emptying my head, not so much. I began to smell sandalwood incense and I let myself give in to its mellowing influence.

When I felt DP's presence, I opened my eyes. He handed me a mug of what smelled like peppermint tea.

"Sip this."

"What's in it?"

"Relax. It'll help you remember."

"The truth is, I'm not sure I want to remember."

"But you need to."

On the table, facing me, he'd set up a projection screen. The image on it caught my attention.

"You recognize that?"

"I think so. That's the Palace Road entrance to the Gardner."

"Was. The day you and your dad visited; you went in that way?"

"Yes. That was the public entrance."

He pulled up a ladder-back chair next to me, straddled it, and folded his arms across the back. He rested his chin on his arms.

"Just the two of you?"

"Yes."

"He didn't take your mom?"

I wondered if my parents were squabbling at the time. That seemed likely.

"No."

"Did your dad take you to museums often? To see art?"

"No. Almost never."

"But he did that day."

I sipped the tea and studied the Gardner's entrance.

"Yes."

"And it was cold."

"Maybe."

"You said it was cold that day."

"Did I?"

"You wanted to play hockey, remember?"

"Yes. That's right."

I summoned the memory.

"On the pond near my house."

"It was cold. Cold enough to skate. You and your dad drove into Boston, and you didn't want to go. He parked the car and the two of you walked together to the museum. Do you remember how cold it was?"

"No."

"What were you wearing?"

"Wait a minute. I remember that I forgot my gloves."

"It was cold. Your hands were stinging."

I sipped more of the tea. I closed my eyes.

"Yes, that's right."

"And you were glad to get inside."

"I was."

He took a sip of his own steaming tea and watched me.

"What did you talk about on the drive to Boston?"

"Probably hockey."

"No. He didn't want to talk about what you were missing out on. He wanted to engage your interest. Did he talk to you about, maybe battle flags and cannons?"

"Why would he do that?"

"You weren't interested in art. You were a kid in your early teens, maybe less. You might have wanted to hear about Napoleon."

My father could spin a tale when the mood was right for him.

"Yes. I remember he talked once about the battle of Waterloo in the car. It could have been that day."

"He said there was a Napoleonic item in the museum."

"He might have."

"There was one thing in the museum associated with Napoleon. It was on the second floor. He wanted to keep you interested, so he took you there right away."

He clicked the projector remote until he got to a slide of the faded French tricolor banner of the Garde Imperiale as it appeared on the day of the theft. Atop the staff was an angry bonze eagle, its wings spread aggressively.

The finial.

I stared at it and closed my eyes. I could see the same picture in my mind, as if it had been imprinted there years and years ago.

The finial.

Yes. This had captured my attention on that cold winter day. Did I say something to my dad about it as I stood before it, imagining cavalry charges and the cannons' roar? Harkening back through the fog of time, I remembered the brick archways and tiled floors of the museum, and I could see his usually impassive face smiling.

"I remember him pointing to it. He was talking about it."

"What did he say?"

Was he anxious that day? What was his attitude? What was he looking at, and why? I wouldn't have noticed any of that back then. I had been bored and distracted that day. I certainly couldn't remember it now.

Except the finial.

"I can see him, DP. I can hear his voice."

I was surprised to recognize his voice in my head, but what I heard was authentic. It was the sound of a childhood that had ended too abruptly. However, it was also a sound that made me hope I could recapture a part of it.

"Joth, the finial and the flag were in what's called the Short Gallery. There were six things taken from there. The finial and five sketches by Edgar Degas."

He clicked to another photo.

"The Short Gallery opens onto the Dutch Room. This is how it looked that day. Six things were taken from this room, too."

I looked at the slide.

"DP, we stopped in front of something else. I can recall a framed painting set up on a table. There were people in the painting. My dad laughed and said, 'How'd you like to see that hanging on the living room wall?'"

He thought for a moment, then clicked on Rembrandt's massive *Storm on the Sea of Galilee*.

"Do you remember this one?"

"Maybe."

"Maybe?"

"No, I don't."

Next up was the Vermeer.

"This is *The Concert*, Joth."

This slide showed a quiet domestic scene from Dutch society: a woman in profile at a harpsichord and a man with his back to the painter, his left hand fingering the strings of a lute. A second woman gestures like one about to sing. Even the picture of the picture was serenely beautiful.

"Any recollection?"

"Yes."

"Do you remember seeing this?"

I searched my memory and dredged up a faded image.

"I do."

He clicked off the projector.

"Did you see the whole museum that day, Joth?"

"What do you mean?"

"Did you go into the basement, for example?"

"I don't know."

"The bathroom was in the basement."

"Alright. I remember that. I was in a hurry to get home, but before we left, he wanted to make sure I had a chance to go, even though I didn't need to. Why?"

"Maybe, just maybe, because the security system was wired into the basement?"

I had realized where this was going, but it still took my breath away to think that my father would use me like that.

"Maybe. Probably. I don't know. But I know he took my brother the next weekend."

I remembered the scene in the kitchen the following Saturday morning.

"Kicking and screaming, I might add."

"How old was your brother?"

"Three years older than me. He was home from boarding school."

"So, he took the two of you on separate trips to the same museum a week or so apart?"

"That's right."

I thought about what Ned and I had discussed before his Saturday morning trip.

"It had to be the next weekend."

"Didn't that strike you as odd?"

"No. Not then. I didn't think that way. I was a kid."

"When was this, Joth? This visit to the Museum?"

"January or February. Maybe March."

"And what year?"

"I don't know."

"Could it have been the winter of 1990?"

I sighed. The window of time between my introduction to hockey and when I moved on to the next thing was brief, like two or three winters.

"Might have been."

DP rested the backs of his fingers against his lips, looked at me and gave me time to reach the obvious conclusion.

"You're trying to say he was casing the place?"

DP nodded.

"Might have been."

"No, I don't think so."

"If someone was casing the museum, isn't that how he would have done it?"

"My father wouldn't have done something like that."

"Of course not."

"It's just a coincidence."

"I thought you didn't believe in coincidences?"

I got up and turned on the lights. It was too much to digest.

"Don't get angry, Joth. It won't help any of this."

DP hadn't hypnotized me, exactly. At least, I didn't think he had. He'd employed a complex methodology for accessing the uncomfortable memories and painful associations that had been gathering dust in my brain for more than two decades. I had never resolved the nagging resentment my father's abandonment had generated. Now, I didn't understand if I should embrace his possible reappearance like an unexpected gift.

"This is enough for one day."

DP nodded. It was enough for a lifetime. There was one thing I hadn't told DP. I knew exactly when my father abandoned the family. It was March 20, 1990, the last day of winter.

I left, walked over to Ireland's Four Courts, and drank myself drunk.

Chapter Twenty-Three

Like a Bad Penny

I didn't sleep well, tossing and turning into the wee hours. When I finally dozed off, I slept so soundly that it was late morning before I awoke. Although I had nothing on my calendar, I went into the office anyway. I acknowledged Marie with a nod, made myself a cup of black coffee, and shut my office door. Then, I slid open the top drawer of my desk. Tucked in the back, among the ticket stubs and letters I had compulsively saved, was a photograph I'd taken of Heather on the DC Mall during the peak of our time together. I took it out and put my feet on the desk as I studied it.

It had been several years since I'd pulled it out and used it to feed my dreams and my misery. She was 27 in the picture and radiant. I had never escaped the power of Heather's allure, but the photograph reminded me of the inevitable wear of time, gradual changes that our regular contact disguised like well-applied make-up. She'd gained weight in the hips and the legs over those years and her still lovely features were no longer as taut and angular. I'd seen the telltale signs of gray in the hair that she kept strawberry colored with periodic trips to the beauty parlor. All that was true, but she remained as intoxicating to me as fine champagne.

It's not my practice to talk through personal problems with anyone, and this is only one of my many failings. It also may help explain why my personal problems are rarely resolved favorably, cleanly, or well.

There were only two people I knew well enough to ask for help on the Heather issue: Irish Dan and DP. Both were trusted business associates and close friends whom I could and did seek out to discuss professional problems of any level of complexity or sensitivity. But neither of them had ever settled into a stable romantic relationship. Any advice they might provide would be drawn from their own speculation or the second-hand anecdotes of the stray cats and opportunists that moved in and out of their lives. What did either of them know of the subtleties and intricacies of love?

This was one of the reasons my father never trusted the clergy for advice on family matters during those frequent times when my parents were reduced to communicating through notes to keep Dad from screaming at Mom and mom from curling up in an emotionally self-protective ball.

All of this turned my thoughts to Father John Tedesco.

At first, this instinctive reaction seemed perverse; a product of my personal cynicism, but the more I thought about it, the clearer the distinction became. This wasn't a challenge of sexual attraction or a problem of cohabitation. It was a matter of human relationship. John would not fall back on the simple but arcane formulations of church doctrine that I had had beaten into me as a youth: "Your faith is not strong enough" or "You need to put your trust in the Lord." Heather was married to another man. Unhappily married, perhaps, but married nonetheless. At its core, it was a question of sin, and my catalogue of substantial sins was already so deep that breaking and entering didn't even crack the list.

It was much too early for the drink I craved, so I decided to settle for another cup of strong coffee while I thought this over. The place to get that was Willard's and the guy to make it was Raighne Youngblood. It was DP who told me that Willard's, a hole-in-the-wall coffee bar, was actually a front for a government safe house. In contrast, almost everyone who ever set foot in that place knew that the mild-mannered Raighne was a disabled combat veteran still recovering from a grievous wound in a sensitive area.

Willard's was empty, as it often is on an early afternoon, and Raighne nodded from behind the bar as he wiped his hands on a soiled white apron. The lights were low in deference to his intolerance of anything bright and the scuffed and scarred dark wood bar faded into the dimness at the far end of the room.

"Something strong and something black."

Raighne nodded again and turned away. With his dark haired and brooding presence, he was not a man to engage in idle chit-chat. I leaned on the bar and waited.

I don't know where Felipe Pasquale came from. He may have been at a table in the shadows at the far end of the room. More likely, he'd been following me, waiting for his chance. All I know is he suddenly appeared behind me, fists clenched, his body coiled with latent aggression.

"Well, look who's here."

His face bore the grim scowl of the executioner he was. I wanted to buy time until I could get a read on him and measure his intentions.

"Hello Felipe."

I had always figured Felipe Pasquale as a guy who'd rely on raw power in a fight. He had plenty of that, but that was alright. I watched him warily, waiting for the first move. I could expect an aggressive, unimaginative approach, and I could parry that. I figured I could take him if I kept my balance and responded to each move without over-committing. But I didn't count on him leading with his left. I was on the floor before I knew what happened.

"Get up."

"I'm not going anywhere."

As he loomed over me, I saw that I had no choice. I struggled to my knees. He took his time and kicked me carefully but forcefully in the side of the face. When I went down this time, I knew I was in trouble, but that was all I knew.

"Get up."

This time, I pushed myself up on one elbow and was just focusing on my surroundings when Felipe pushed me down and I felt his powerful hands on my throat. Then, in a flash, I sensed rather than saw a whirlwind of fists and feet that left Felipe on the floor next to me, groaning.

Somebody helped me to a sitting position. It was Raighne, the purportedly emasculated barista. I fought to capture my breath, and as I did, I felt a warm rush of thick, viscous liquid pulsing out beneath my right eye. Raighne staunched it with a towel.

"Can you get to your feet?"

I looked over at the wheezing pile of flesh that was Felipe.

"I think so."

I took the towel from Raighne and pressed it to my cheek. With his help, I stood up and took a deep breath.

"You better get out before the police get here."

"Why don't I . . .?"

He silenced me with a fingertip to my chest and a stern look.

"It would be better."

"What are you going to tell them?"

Raighne shrugged and looked at Felipe.

"The truth. That he got into a tussle with a customer and that the other guy got away."

I felt the cut throbbing under my eye.

"You sure about this?"

"Trust me. Don't get involved."

I took the towel and staggered outside into the leafy, residential neighborhood west of Wilson Boulevard. I concentrated on maintaining a steady gait as a method of pulling myself together and kept walking until I found an iron bench in a pocket park. I sat down to catch my breath and consider my options. I knew I needed some-one to look at the bleeding cut beneath my eye. My first thought was DP. I called but he didn't pick up. Heather was next, but she would have questions I wasn't sure I wanted to answer. I could only think of one other person. She answered on the first ring.

I heard the low hum of conversation behind her. It was too early for her shift at the assisted living facility where she worked.

"Hi Melanie. I had a little accident."

"Are you alright?"

"I don't know. I'm bleeding."

She must have heard more in my strained tone. Her voice dropped to a whisper, but she sounded calm.

"I'll pick you up. Where are you?"

I squinted up at the street signs and gave her the location.

"I'll be right there."

Melanie drove a boxy little electric car and she pulled it up to the curb with a wheeze. Wearing tight-fitting jeans and a purple sweater, I imagined her as a descending angel in the kind of baroque painting that still hung in the Gardner.

"What happened?"

"I walked into a lamp post."

That didn't fool her. It wasn't supposed to, but she stopped asking questions. Instead, she helped me into the passenger seat and drove me quickly to the Virginia Hospital Center, double parking in the horseshoe driveway in front of the Emergency Room.

"Thanks, Melanie."

She came around the car and took my arm in hers to guide me inside to the ER.

It was a short visit. I told the doc the same thing I had told Melanie and she didn't believe me either. She numbed the injured area with a shot of Novocaine, then backed away, cleaning her glasses while it took effect.

"You know, we have an obligation to report suspicious injuries to the police."

"There's nothing here to report."

"Then, tell me the truth."

She was a slim woman of medium height with blonde hair and the high complexion of someone of Nordic descent. Her name plate read "Dr. Terry" and she watched me like a hawk.

"Okay. I got into a fight."

"With your domestic partner?"

"I don't have a domestic partner. It was an old teammate. We were horsing around, and it got out of hand. I slipped and banged my face on the mantlepiece."

She still didn't believe me. She'd seen me come in on the arm of a woman with a concerned look on her face.

"Let's give that medicine a minute or two to work," she said.

She left me seated on the gurney while she went out to the hall and shut the door behind her. I knew what she was doing. She was questioning Melanie.

When she came back a minute or two later, she was all business as she stitched me up.

"You're going to have a little scar here. You can address it with over-the-counter scar cream that you can get in any drug store."

I tuned out the rest of her lecture. A little scar was the least of my concerns.

I don't know how Jimmie found out what happened, but he arrived just as I was coming out of the emergency room with eight stitches in my face. Melanie had just taken my arm. He unlinked hers from mine and took me firmly by the elbow.

"You're coming with me."

Melanie shrunk away, looking at me in shock. Jimmie was usually carefully dressed, if not dapper, but now he looked like someone had wakened him up from a nap, which increased his air of menace. I don't know why I gave in to him, but I did. Jimmie had that way with people.

"It's okay, Melanie," I said. "He's a friend."

We'd walked several unsteady steps when the sound of a shrill and earsplitting whistle ripped through the atrium of the hospital and momentarily silenced everyone within earshot. I turned toward the sound. It was Melanie, who stood with her hands on her hips.

"Thanks, Joth."

"For what?"

"For making it easy on me. For reminding me what a self-absorbed son of a bitch you are."

I didn't have a response. Jimmie looked at me and shrugged.

Jimmie drove a metallic blue Corvette, and on his calmest days he drove it like a man in a hurry. On this day, his intense manner betrayed a concern that went beyond his usual impatience, and he sped recklessly, passing cars through a series of no-passing zones.

"You look fine."

"I'm sure."

"This is on me. If you need plastic surgery, I'll make the arrangements."

"Do you know where he is? Felipe, I mean?"

"He's in jail."

I sighed and relaxed.

"Good place for him."

"No, it's not."

Jimmie took me straight to his office. It was a short drive but enough time for me to work through the fog and for Jimmie to regain his poise. We sat in his reception area, where the chair he offered me was marginally more comfortable than the stiff and thinly padded seat across from the desk in his inner office. Helen stood up when we came in and her fingers went to her cheekbones. She seemed equally unsettled by my face and her boss's bedraggled appearance. The ER doc had given me two prescriptions and Jimmie sent her out to get them filled. After she left, he took the chair behind the reception desk. The room felt cramped, steamy, and claustrophobic and I could not understand why he brought me there.

"I've got vodka and whiskey."

My ribs ached more than my face, I had a hell of a headache, and I could still feel Felipe's fingers on my throat.

"Water will be fine."

He ignored my answer and seemed to forget about his offer.

"Jimmie, when did you find out Felipe was back in town?"

"Not until after you did. I heard you did a number on him."

"Who told you that?"

"I've got my sources."

Of course, it was Raighne who'd done a number on Felipe, but I wasn't going to disabuse him. A healthy dose of physical fear would be a valuable tool in my ongoing battle with Jimmie Flambeau, so I let the rumor stand.

206

I had taken a towel from the hospital, and Jimmy watched me use it to make sure the bleeding had stopped.

"You got any ice?"

"Helen will get you some."

I dabbed some more at my swollen cheek.

"You said he's in jail? Felipe, I mean?"

"Yes, he's in jail. And that's the problem."

"Problem? It sounds like the solution to me."

"He's eligible for bond. You need to get him bonded out."

"What are you talking about?"

"You got any idea what he could say about me and my operation? A guy like that is only going to be quiet for so long before he sees the wisdom of singing."

Jimmie pounded the desk with his fist.

"He's charged with assaulting that barista at Willard's. It's only a misdemeanor. He's entitled to bond. I need you to get in front of a magistrate and get him the hell out of there before they start putting big pressure on him!"

I'd heard several preposterous demands from Jimmie Flambeau, but nothing like this. I was witnessing something I had never seen before. Jimmie Flambeau was scared because an out-of-control simpleton who knew where all the bodies were buried might be getting ready to talk to the police.

"Get him out? Come on, Jimmie. You want me to argue a bond motion for the guy who put me in the hospital?"

I didn't mention that I was in no shape to appear in court, but I knew that would be a waste of my limited supply of breath.

"Nobody knows that."

Raighne Youngblood did. And as far as I knew, he worked for the Commonwealth.

"Not only that; Felipe just got indicted for killing Nick Grimes. How long do you think it'll be before those two warrants get matched up?"

Jimmie looked at me sharply. None of this was lost on him.

"You're wasting your time, Jimmie. And besides, the guy might have killed me."

"I can get somebody else, you know."

"Go ahead."

Then I asked the question I really wanted answered.

"If he gets out, then what. What happens to Felipe?"

"You don't need to worry. I'll take possession of him."

"Goddam it, Jimmie. Get me some ice!"

He did. He got up like a host who'd suddenly re-membered his manners and brought me a plastic cup with four cubes in it. I wrapped them in the towel and held it to my swollen cheek.

"Felipe's a problem, Jimmie, but not one that I can help you with."

He didn't argue. He knew I was right, and as he turned away I could see the wheels turning in his head.

When Helen returned with the prescriptions, his mood mellowed. I took one of each pill with the glass of water she'd graciously brought in and put the two plastic containers in my pocket.

"I'm going home to bed. If Felipe's still in jail tomorrow, we'll talk about it then."

I should have known he wouldn't be.

Chapter Twenty-Four

Background Check

It was Ish who called to warn me. The incessant buzzing of my cellphone woke me in the dark of night. Fuzzy-headed, I looked at my watch: 2:30.

"Felipe Pasquale just got out of jail."

I recognized the voice and the news brought me to my feet.

"Got out? He made bond?"

Ish's voice was calm and alert. I assumed he was on duty in the jail.

"No, but he's out."

"How did that happen?"

"A paperwork mix-up. That's what they're saying, anyway. They released the wrong guy."

"Released the wrong guy?"

"It happens."

I wondered how he knew about my connection to Felipe, but Ish was a man who kept his ear to the ground. I got up and called Jimmie, mostly because I wanted the small measure of satisfaction I'd get from waking him with bad news in the middle of the night.

Jimmie was wide awake and unsurprised and now I understood what had happened to Felipe. Paperwork mix ups were rare, but they weren't always the result of honest mistakes made by jail administrators under the pressure of time.

"Do you know where Felipe is now?"

"Don't worry about it, Joth. It's under control. Go back to sleep."

I crawled back in bed. I took another pill, but I couldn't sleep or even find a comfortable position to rest in. I didn't doubt that Jimmie had the thing under control. It disturbed me more than a little bit to speculate about what that might mean.

I found Father John Tedesco's number in my phone and called him. Priests were first responders as far as I was concerned, trained to handle desperate calls made in the darkest hours. He answered quickly, but the sound of my voice unsettled him. He took a moment to get his bearings.

"This can't be good, Joth."

"It's not. You got any unused vacation time?"

He didn't seem to understand the question.

"Felipe Pasquale tried to kill me today. I'm worried you might be on his list, too."

"He's back?"

John sounded terrified and I was sure he was.

"Why don't you take a drive out to the Valley for a few days until this blows over?"

"I don't know, Joth. I'll have to speak to the diocese."

"Well, do yourself a favor and call them from the road."

No response.

"John, I'll sleep a lot better if you get in your car and get going. Please."

"Alright. I can leave in two hours."

"Make it an hour, John. Anything you forget, you can pick up on the road."

He agreed.

Having done what I needed to do, I dozed off. When the rising sun woke me again, I felt rested enough to get back to work. San Diego hadn't been far enough away, and Jimmie's assurance that Felipe was off the grid wasn't good enough for me. Pasquale was a psychopath, a man without the capacity to experience or share emotions. His tendency to violence sprang from a need to experience them vicariously, and it seemed that I was his current instrument of fulfillment. I wondered about the poor girl in Delaware he had killed Nicholas Grimes over. I hoped somebody was looking out for her.

But it wasn't Pasquale that got me on my feet. It was the prospect of recovering some of the Gardner art. I threw on a tweed sport coat and went down to see Irish Dan.

Dan's moods usually ranged from ebullient to sullen with little in between, and as he saw me walk toward him, his face brightened. He was nodding approvingly at the sport coat I was wearing when he noticed my black eye and the eight-stitch cut.

"I was going to say you look pretty fashionable but what happened? You look like hell, Joth."

"I feel worse. How's it going with the two pips?"

Dan waved his hands.

"They're off limits. Even to you."

"You got 'em working yet?"

"No, they're still studying English, but Dapper says they're almost ready. Beer or coffee?"

"A little early for beer, isn't it?"

"Not around here."

He took the hint and filled a pair of white ceramic mugs from the coffee urn behind the bar. He put them on a tray along with sugar, cream and spoons, then he nodded toward the line of empty booths. I took the side facing the door, just in case.

After we sat down, he pushed a mug across to me and added sugar and cream to his.

"Speaking of Dapper, you see much of him?"

"Not much; now that you mention it. It's a busy time of year. When Congress is in session, this place seems like an auxiliary caucus room. You get him an immigration lawyer?"

"Sure did."

"How's that going?"

"He didn't hire her."

He sipped loudly.

"Didn't hire her? How come?"

"I guess he didn't like her."

"Did you fix him up with somebody else?"

"He didn't ask."

Dan glanced at the upright piano and scowled. He was paying the two pips on Dapper's promise to obtain their green cards, and that wouldn't happen unless Dapper got an immigration lawyer involved. This may have sounded like a breach of faith to Dan. It sounded that way to me, too.

"Maybe you can start using them around here."

Dan knew better than that. He wasn't risk averse, but he carefully calculated the chances he took and gambled only when he smelled a significant upside. He wasn't going to risk his business by employing illegal aliens in any capacity. And Dan had known me long enough to see that I was working around to something else. He cocked his head at me and waited.

"How well do you really know McNair?"

"Just what he told me."

"That's what I thought. I'm surprised you were so quick to trust him."

"For one thing, he says he knows your family."

"Except I'm not sure that he does."

"Really? He seems like a decent guy."

"Dan, some of the stuff he says just doesn't add up."

He put the mug down in front of him and folded his hands.

"Like what?"

"For one thing, I don't think Dapper McNair's his real name."

He shrugged.

"Dapper's probably a nickname."

"I'm betting McNair is, too."

"What's his game then?"

"Trying to foist those girls off on you, for one thing."

"That's a lot of trouble for a couple of immigrants who don't speak English."

"If that's who they really are."

Dan held my eyes for a long moment. I could see the wheels turning, and I wasn't sure I wanted to know what he was thinking.

"What are you going to do, Joth?"

"This McNair, or whoever he is, is slandering my family name. One of the oldest families in Massachusetts. I don't know why, but I'm sure it's got to do with money. And I'm going to find out."

"That usually means trouble for somebody."

"I'll make sure it's not you."

"What's the first step?"

"Maybe it's time for me to have a talk with the two pips."

"They're nice girls, Joth."

"I'm sure. Can you give me their address?"

He hesitated, but I had come through for Dan too many times. He jotted it down with a black sharpie on a soiled cork coaster. I made sure I could read it and put in in my pocket. I looked at my watch.

"Think they'll be home?"

"They better be. I'm paying them to learn English."

Chapter Twenty-Five

The Mixed Pair from Brockton

The address Dan had given me was a two-story duplex close to the street, with white aluminum siding that looked like it had endured all that nature could throw at it and was pugnaciously ready for the next round. Two sets of granite stairs, three steps each, led up to the two entrances. The one on the right belonged to the royal pips.

After taking a careful look around, I stepped into a narrow, weedy side yard strewn with fast food wrappers. It was a warm, damp day and a first-floor window was open. I kicked a dead rat to the concrete slab and stood next to the window, listening to a pair of low, subdued voices and the blare of a television. The TV was too loud to make out the voices, but the language was recognizable, and they weren't watching *Star Wars*.

Dapper's story was already leaking air.

I went back to the front and quietly mounted the stairs. The door was unlocked. I pushed it open and stepped inside a small room furnished with a grubby couch and two chairs facing a big screen TV. The two young women were facing away from me. I walked toward them until they heard me and turned at the same time, both startled. The girl to my right stood up, her pale, pretty face animated, perplexed and anxious. The other one sat insouciantly in a battered, lime green armchair. I stepped forward, picked up the remote, and turned off the TV.

"My name is Joth Proctor. I work with Dan Crowley. I'm here to tell you that this gig is over, girls. The good news is that Dan's got one job opening, tending bar at the sports pub. Whoever speaks up first gets it. The other one's out."

No response, but the girl with the pale face looked rattled. It might have been the cut and the black eye, but I didn't think so. I took a conspicuous look at my watch.

"It's three. I'll be back in twenty-four hours to get your answer. If neither one of you wants that job, you both better have your stuff out of here by then, because I'm bringing a locksmith. Any questions?"

The one on my left, olive-skinned and slender and dressed in leather pants and a tight red top, occupied herself by shaking out and lighting a cigarette. The pale-faced girl, bigger bodied than the other, wore a Tom Brady jersey and a pair of gray sweats with the Patriots logo on the hip. She watched me as she kneaded her hands. Neither one of them said a word.

I turned and walked back to the door. As I stepped out to the stoop, my hand still on the knob, one of them spoke,

"Wait a minute."

***

Their names were Pam and Nancy Herrick and they spoke English with the distinct Boston accent I was familiar with from my youth. They were both blonde, but blonde from a bottle. I asked them for their driver's licenses and Pam, the pale one, reached for her purse. Nancy ignored me, blowing perfect smoke rings toward the ceiling.

Pam did the talking. She would become heavy before too many more years passed, but now she was in her prime. She had blue eyes and an innocent smile with soft, amiable features. I snapped my fingers and held out my hand and she fished a Massachusetts driver's license out of her purse. I looked at the photo and up at her. Pam Herrick's license showed a photograph of the woman I was looking at and listed an address in Brockton, Massachusetts.

"How 'bout you?"

Nancy turned toward me for the first time.

"I'll take that job."

She was a striking woman, with high cheek bones and a thin, aquiline nose. I waited her out and she handed me her license with something close to a snarl. Same last name, same address, same birthdate. They were sisters alright, but everything else Dapper McNair had told Dan Crowley about them was a lie.

"Twins?"

"Fraternal," said Pam. "Different eggs. That's why we don't look alike."

I could already see that her sister was the hard boiled one.

"Who's older?"

Pam raised her hand.

"I am."

The other one tsked.

"Fifteen minutes."

I sat on the couch. Pam turned her chair toward me and sat down.

"How did Dapper run you two down?"

Pam snuck a glance at her sister and took a breath.

"Well, it's a long story."

It wasn't really. They both had been in the management training program at a McDonald's in Brockton, a working-class suburb south of Boston. Dapper, who had some sort of business in the area, came in often for lunch. Except his name wasn't Dapper then. It was David.

"David what?"

Pam shook her head.

"I don't know. Nancy said Taylor, but she also said that wasn't his real name."

"Taylor's his real last name," Nancy said. "He told me."

"She should know," said Pam. "She's sleeping with him."

"Not anymore."

I took another look at Nancy's license before giving it back to her.

"You ever see his driver's license?"

"You think we card people for ordering a big Mac?" Nancy said.

The Herrick sisters were twenty-four years old. Dapper, aka David, had to have more than a quarter century on them. Nonetheless, I didn't doubt that Nancy had been sleeping with him if she'd seen him as her way out of Brockton. I pegged her as pugnacious and willing to take chances. She was also feisty.

"What did you say your name was?" she said.

"Proctor."

"John Proctor?"

"Joth. Joth Proctor."

Nancy looked at her sister, but Pam's face was blank.

"I thought you'd look older."

"I'm pretty damn old. Which one's the pianist?"

Nancy's eyes blinked several times. Pam raised her hand like an obedient schoolgirl.

"And you're going to play harpsichord in Dan's place?"

"Why not?" said Nancy. "Unless something better comes up."

"There was some talk about a concert," said Pam.

She looked at her sister, as if she had said too much. I noticed that whenever Pam looked at Nancy, it seemed as if she were looking for a signal. When Nancy looked at Pam, she was delivering a message.

I turned to Nancy.

"And you're the pastry chef? How did you come to acquire those skills?"

Pam glanced at her sister, but Nancy was back to blowing smoke rings. Pam was the weak link, so I spoke to her.

"I'll bet this whole thing was your idea."

She shook her head vehemently.

"David. Everything was his idea."

"How'd he get you two to come down here?"

"The money was decent, plus it's a good place to live. And it's far away from Brockton."

"Do you understand what he got you into?"

Pam's face lit up in alarm.

"Don't say anything, Pam."

Nancy blew out more smoke and crossed her legs.

"Alright, we're not getting anywhere like this. I'll give you a day to think it over. When I come back tomorrow, I want the whole truth. The two of you are stuck in the middle of something pretty messy. I can get you out of this without involving the police, but you're working for me now, not David. And don't forget that Dan's still paying you, but he'll cut that off as soon as I tell him to."

It was damp outside, and a fog was beginning to develop. I took a last careful look at the two sisters: one defiant, the other anxious and eager to please. Giving them a day to contemplate their vulnerable situation would produce a more cooperative attitude. At least that's what I thought.

Chapter Twenty-Six

Dead Blonde in the Alley

I knew about the man who came to be called the Crystal City Choker before almost anyone else, even before the press gave him the name. I heard about it from Irish Dan because it was one of the pips who'd been strangled.

It was not yet five in the morning when my phone rang. Dan, who was always as steady as a lighthouse in a high wind, sounded frantic and uncharacteristically emotional.

"It's murder Joth, and right down the street. Right on Fern Street!"

He was crying. The sound of my old friend in distress unnerved me but I knew he'd called for support.

"Someone you know?"

"Someone you know!"

He continued sobbing.

"Yvonne Wonderlace. It's Yvonne. I just identified her body."

"I'll be right there, Dan."

The thick fog diffused the early morning light and rubberneckers among the commuter traffic had brought 23rd Street to a standstill. The crime scene was just up the street from Riding Time and yellow police tape fenced off an entire block on the north side of Fern Street. I elbowed my way through the gathering crowd until I felt a forceful hand on my chest. It was Dak Commito, a homicide detective and a friend, to the extent I could call any cop a friend. Police photographers and forensic experts were working the scene.

"I'm looking for Dan."

"He told me to look for you. He'll be in his office."

I turned again and took in the grim scene.

"What can you tell me, Dak?"

"Not much. Poor kid was strangled, although you didn't hear that from me."

"How long ago?"

"Six or seven hours, best guess."

I wondered what Yvonne could have been doing down here at that time.

"Dan thinks I might have known her."

"Yeah, I know. He told me. You want to see her before we take her up?"

I took a breath. I wasn't sure if Yvonne was Pam or Nancy.

"I guess I better."

They had her laid out in a gurney in an ambulance parked on a side street. I stepped into the back and was greeted by the repulsive stench of body fluids and the first waves of physical corruption. An EMT looked at me, then pulled the sheet back. It was Pam, her pale complexion now as sickly white as the underside of a cod. Her pretty face was frozen in an expression of pain and horror, her throat black and blue in the stark light inside the ambulance.

I nodded and the tech put the sheet back over her. I stumbled my way through a silent prayer and clapped Dak on his muscular shoulder as I scrambled out.

"Robbed?"

"Hard to tell. Somebody went through her purse, but all the usual contents are still there. Cash and credit cards weren't touched."

"The killer was looking for something?"

"Seems like it."

I looked at what he'd laid out and in the open purse.

"No phone?"

"Maybe she didn't have one."

"Or the killer took it."

Dak nodded.

"That would tend to mean he knew her."

"Or he wants you to think that. How did you know to call Dan?"

Dak pointed to Dan's business card among the collection of her personal items.

"She work for him?"

"I'm not sure."

I wasn't ready to divulge anything yet.

"She doesn't look like the type, Joth."

I looked again at her clean, innocent face, so disfigured by this brutal murder.

"No, she doesn't."

"Anything you can tell me?"

"If I were you, Dak, I'd be looking for a big, semi-illiterate psychopath. His name is Felipe Pasquale."

Commito turned to measure my expression. It looked like he hadn't connected Pasquale to the crime, but I knew he would, given time, with or without my help.

"The guy who just walked out of the Arlington jail?"

"That's the guy."

He nodded and peered closely at me.

"Works for Flambeau, doesn't he?"

"Used to. Flambeau cut him loose a while ago."

"Any idea where we can find him?"

"I wish I knew. There's a warrant out for him in that banker's murder."

"Grimes?"

"Yeah, that's the guy."

"If we're looking for him anyway, it shouldn't take long."

I shook Dak's hand, and he took a good look at the fresh bruise and cut on my face.

"Who gave you that?"

"Nobody you know."

"Well, be careful."

"Keep me posted, will you, Dak?"

Out on the street, I put my hands on my hips and sucked in the chilly morning air. I couldn't be sure if Pasquale had killed Pam, but it seemed like a good bet. Everyone getting killed in Arlington seemed to have a connection to him and that needed to end. Dak said he would keep me in the loop, and I believed him. Commito was kind of a hothead, but he was a straight-shooter and reliable.

***

When I got to Riding Time, the front door was closed and the lacy curtain that covered the front window was pulled tight. There was a hand-written sign on the door that read "Closed Until Further Notice." I went around back and worked the combination to let myself in the service door.

227

Dan took a paternal interest in all the girls who worked for him. I figured a talk would help him work through the terrible news and that I'd find him brooding in his office. I was wrong. The overhead lights were on in the main room, but set on dim, casting a dull illumination over the long, narrow space. Dan sat at the big table in front of the main stage. He was drinking. I dragged one of the chairs around so I could sit across from him. When he looked up at me, his eyes were puffy and red.

"This is a tough morning, Joth."

"It is. Did you break it to the sister?"

Dan shook his head.

"I was hoping you'd talk to her."

"Do the cops have Yvonne's address?"

"Whatever's on her driver's license."

I already knew what was on her driver's license. Anybody looking for her in Massachusetts wouldn't find her, including Pasquale, if that's what he had in mind.

I slipped my fingers around Dan's drink, pulled it toward me and sniffed: whiskey on the rocks.

"I'm going to get myself a cup of coffee. I'll get you one, too."

They prep the urn every night at closing time and all I had to do was push the button. As it began to wheeze and gurgle, I poured Dan's cocktail down the drain.

Connecting the murder to Pasquale hadn't occurred to Commito. Maybe he was right. The dead girl was hooked up with McNair and the more I learned about Dapper, the less I liked him. I was willing to break the news to Nancy, but there were things I needed from Dan first. I went back to sit with him while the coffee brewed.

He hadn't moved. His head was still bowed over folded hands.

"What do you want me to tell her?"

"How 'bout that her twin sister's dead?"

"Dan, don't you think she's going to have questions?"

"Questions I can't answer."

"You might be able to answer some of them."

He didn't respond. I got back up and went behind the bar to give time for my comment to germinate. While the coffee brewed, I found two clean cups and put sugar and cream in Dan's, then filled them both, one at a time, directly from the dripping urn. I carried both to the table and put Dan's in front of him. He ignored it.

"They strangled her, Joth."

"I know. I saw her."

"Who would have done something like that?"

It was a good time to test my second theory.

"Dapper McNair comes to mind. Or whatever his real name is."

Dan looked up, shocked by the suggestion.

"You don't think he had anything to do with this?"

My focus on McNair had been limited to stolen paintings and what he might be saying about my father, but now I wondered if the killer wanted the same thing as Dapper. Could Pam have obtained some compromising knowledge about the stolen art? Perhaps she'd learned more than was convenient and was ready to use it. I didn't think so, but it was possible.

"I don't know, but I'm going to run that down this morning."

"I think Dapper had something going on with the sister."

"Had?"

"I think so."

"So, maybe he had tried to move on to Pam, and she resisted?"

Dan shook his head.

"I get a lot of semi-bad men come in and out of this place. Con men, grifters, congressmen. You know the type, people looking for an edge, looking for a buck. But a brutal, cold-blooded killer? I didn't see McNair that way."

I allowed that idea to percolate in my mind. I agreed that extreme violence didn't seem consistent with the character of the man I had met, but he was a hard case.

Dan sometimes trusted the wrong people, but he had a nice sense for a man's true nature. Dan's instincts were a factor in McNair's favor.

I nudged the coffee in front of Dan the way you nudge a bowl of food in front of an ailing dog. He took the hint and took a long drink. It seemed to help.

I looked at the clock over the bar. Just past seven. As Dan said, it was a tough morning, and it was going to get worse. I needed to get started.

"Okay, Dan, I'll go up and see the sister. I'll let you know how that goes. Then, I'm going to spend some time with McNair."

I knew which conversation would be more difficult. I wondered if the second one would at least provide some answers.

***

Dan gave me the phone number of the young woman he knew as Eva and I knew as Nancy, and as I walked toward her duplex, I thought about calling, just to give her a chance to get out of bed and wake up. But she'd have questions I couldn't answer on the phone.

Instead, I knocked loudly and insistently on the front door, both to get her up and to communicate the urgency of the message I was there to deliver. She came to the door wrapped in a short green bathrobe of faux silk, her blonde hair tousled with sleep. She was one of those rare women who is more beautiful in her natural state than when she's fully put together. As she opened the door, she instinctively began tightening the cinch of her robe, but she stopped when she saw it was me.

"This can't be good."

"It's not. Can I come in?"

"Okay."

She turned away and started for the stairs.

"I'll get Pam."

"Pam's not home, Nancy."

She stopped and spun around to face me, her eyes and mouth wide in an expression close to fear.

"We'd better sit down."

As she sat in the lime green armchair, I took the same seat Pam had occupied on my previous visit. Nancy loosened the sash on her bathrobe. There was nothing lascivious in the gesture. This was a woman who'd heard enough bad news in her life that she knew when it was coming. She threw her head back and steadied herself.

"How bad is it?"

"Very bad. As bad as it can be."

There was a pack of Camels on the table beside her. She shook one out, but it took several flicks of her thumb on the lighter to bring it to life. She sucked in deeply and blew out the smoke. I watched her add up all that she'd heard so far, processing the facts that I had parceled out.

"She's dead isn't she?"

"Yes."

"Accident?"

"I'm afraid not."

She nodded, struggling to maintain her composure.

"Who did it?"

"We don't know."

"Where's Dapper?"

"That's my next stop. You don't think . . ."

"No. Not a chance. It was a complicated relationship, I guess, but he loved us both in his own weird way."

"Had Pam made any enemies or friends down here?"

Nancy let the thought drift away. Pam was dead and it didn't matter at this moment who did it.

"No."

She shifted her posture, and it was apparent that she was wearing next to nothing under her robe. As she moved, one of her small, perfectly formed breasts emerged from her robe. A red rose was tattooed on the smooth skin across the top. When she noticed, she covered it with a careless and unapologetic gesture. She was past the point of concerning herself with social niceties.

"And Dapper?"

I waited for her to focus on my question, and she quickly came back to it.

"He used to come by a lot more at first. I'm not saying he started to trust us, but he felt he could leave us alone."

"Dapper's sick, isn't he?"

"Yes, he is. Has been sick since we met him."

What's wrong with him, exactly?"

"Cirrhosis of the liver. That's what he says. It's probably true."

"Big drinker?"

She shrugged.

"No more than a lot of people I know. He thought it was the rot gut he got in prison that did it to him."

"Why was he in prison?'

"Robbed an armored car. He got thirty years."

"That seems like a lot of time for a robbery. Even armed."

She shrugged.

"He brought a hand grenade with him. At least that's what the government said."

I remembered that Dapper told me he'd been set up.

"I see. Did she go out much? Your sister?"

"No. We didn't socialize. That was part of the deal. Our paychecks depended on us toeing the line, you know, and it was easy money. Pam bought the groceries.

We split the kitchen duties. We cooked for Dapper when he wasn't up to it. Ran whatever little errands he needed us to do. Like I said, it was easy money."

Nancy was a tough nut, but the recollection of their domestic arrangement choked her up.

"Let me get you a glass of water."

What I really wanted was to give her a moment to get herself back together. I walked into the kitchen where there was a stack of dirty dishes in the sink. I found a glass, cleaned it, filled it with cold tap water, and brought it back in. Nancy held it in both hands with thanks and took a grateful sip. Then, the cigarette was back in her mouth.

"Nancy, it looks like she was killed around midnight. What would she have been doing out at that hour?"

It took her a moment; then she shook her head.

"Only thing I can think of is Dapper might have needed something."

"Did he call her late at night?"

"He sometimes did."

"How come he called her and not you?"

"Pam is nicer than me."

She emitted a quick sob.

"Was."

She shook her head and blew a smoke ring at the ceiling. I saw that I was running close to some rough water.

"I'm very sorry, Nancy. Did you hear her get up last night?"

"No, but I'm a sound sleeper. You talk to Dapper?"

"No, that's my next stop."

She nodded. She was smoking furiously.

"Can I see her?"

"I can take you down if you like."

She hesitated.

"Nancy, it's going to be kind of ugly."

"What happened?"

"Somebody strangled her."

At last, the tears came and I let her cry it out. I gave her a few minutes, then walked over, took her by her slender shoulders and stood her up.

"Listen, I'm going to give you some time. You take a shower, get dressed, and get something in your stomach. I'll be back to get you in an hour."

"Okay."

I was surprised by the level of compassion and protectiveness I felt for Nancy Herrick.

"You just stay put, Nancy."

"Thanks, John."

"Joth."

"John," she said again.

She saw something on my face that confused her.

"John Proctor, right?"

"I'm not John Proctor. I'm Joth Proctor."

"Then who's John Proctor?"

"My father."

I expected her to get cagey at this point, but she didn't.

"John Proctor. That's what David said."

I sat down.

Nancy had only taken a first sip from the glass of water I'd brought back from the kitchen for her. I picked it up and drained it.

"Keep the door locked, okay?"

She nodded and quietly thanked me as I let myself out.

Chapter Twenty-Seven

Witness Protection

I stepped outside. A light breeze had come up and the fog was lifting, but I could see that the day would remain overcast. The leaves were growing brittle with the cooler weather and the breeze that rattled the trees dissipated some of the grim tension that had been building since Dan woke me up.

I had agreed to give Nancy an hour to get ready because I needed to see Dapper or David or whatever his name really was. Nancy had confirmed Dan's opinion: McNair might be a lot of things, but he wasn't a killer. But I'd been wrong so often lately that I was glad to have a chance to confirm my assumption. A lot of questions remained, and I believed McNair had most of the answers. Whether he was going to give them to me was another issue.

I knew from our first meeting that Dapper McNair was a late riser and I expected to find him at home at nine on a weekday morning. It was faster to walk to his place than it would have been to drive. The walk also allowed me to approach the little bungalow down a side street that screened me from the front windows and driveway, where I saw McNair's aging Lincoln.

I waited a minute or two, then slipped quietly onto the porch and peered into the windows. Nothing. No lights, no signs of life. I tried the door. Locked. I banged away, much as I had at Nancy's house. No response. Maybe he was sleeping off a late night? Feeling the effects of his illness? I got no answer when I called his cell.

Something wasn't right but figuring that out would have to wait.

I got an egg sandwich at a diner on the way back to Nancy's and called ahead to let the morgue know that I was on the way and bringing the next of kin.

I got to Nancy's around ten. She was waiting for me just inside the door. Dressed in tight jeans and a brown turtleneck sweater, she looked as good as a woman can who'd just heard that her twin sister had been murdered.

"You talk to Dapper?"

"He wasn't home."

"Not home? That's weird."

I thought so, too, but I didn't tell her that.

In the car, she left her seatbelt unfastened until the repeated warning chimes demanded that she buckle it. As we drove, she fidgeted, dreading the moment to come.

"I'll be glad to get this goddamn dye out of my hair," she said.

I snuck a look at her profile, the smooth complexion, the elegant nose.

"What color is your hair?"

"Brown. Light brown."

I imagined her with light brown hair. I could see that it would enhance her natural coloring and pick up her brown eyes. It was an attractive picture, and I knew I would have trouble shaking it. For the moment, it was a welcome distraction. I wasn't in the habit of visiting morgues to identify dead bodies.

"I'm not sure I understand how Dapper, or David, got you down here."

"You ever been to Brockton?"

"Sure. That's where you used to go to get shoes."

"Shoes. Shoes and boxers. My father started as a boxer. He ended up in the mill. That's where he met my mom. I didn't want that. Neither did Pam."

"What was David offering?"

"He said he'd take care of us and he did. He may not look like it, but the guy's a real sweetheart and he has plenty of big ideas. He was offering us something better, or at least something different."

"So, he conned you?"

"Not at all. He wasn't fooling anybody. It was just a chance to get out. And we'd be together, Pam and me."

"So, it was a two-person deal?"

"I wasn't going without Pam. I told him that."

"The piano?"

"That part's legit. She was ready. She just needed the opportunity."

I tried to imagine their youth in Brockton.

"Pam got piano lessons. What did you get?"

"I got a harmonica."

She laughed to show that this was a joke.

"She's the older sister, so that's how that goes."

"That must have bothered you some."

"At first, yeah, but piano lessons would have been wasted on me. Pam was the good kid. Always doing the right thing. And she could really play."

Nancy paused and looked out the window, raising a finger to wipe something off her cheek. I gave her a moment. I figured her emotions must be all over the place at a time like this, shocked and lost one second and in denial the next.

"Pam said there was some talk about a concert."

"That was David. Big plans! He was in a band before he went to prison, and he said he still had contacts in the music business. He said he could get her top end work down here, but the best he could do for a start was a novelty act in a sports pub."

"How did John Proctor fit into that?"

She shrugged.

"I don't know. Sometimes, if he'd been drinking, stuff would spill out of David's mouth."

"Stuff like what?"

"Stuff like David and John Proctor used to be in a band together. If he's really your father, you must know more about it than I do."

That made no sense. My father was a hardheaded man of business with no interest in music.

"But this scam with the Wonderlace sisters. What did you know about that?"

She shrugged.

"It was a game to us, you know? It was almost like a vacation. We both knew he was up to something but we knew better than to ask."

"Did he ever mention anything about art? About paintings?"

She turned to look at me.

"What paintings?"

She was playing it coy and that bothered me.

"Come on, Nancy. The ones that were stolen from the Isabella Stewart Gardner."

"I heard about it. I mean, who hasn't up home?"

"Let's talk about the Gardner. What did David say about it?"

She thought about her answer, then softened.

"He said he knew where some of the stuff was and he thought he could get his hands on it. That's all. It didn't mean any more to me than the Wonderlace sisters thing."

I weighed this information as I drove. She wasn't easy to figure out. She might be a simple girl from Brockton, just wanting anything better than what she had, but I couldn't shake the idea that she was hiding something.

"Did David say how he found out? About the paintings, I mean."

"He's known for years. He was inside for a long time. Walpole. I already told you that. He heard stuff in there, but he had to wait until he got out to do anything with it. He didn't like talking about it."

"He didn't mind talking to me about it. He told me he planned the whole thing."

"The Gardner job?"

"Yes."

She laughed.

"Does he look like a guy who could pull off something like that?"

There was some truth to that, but he was a young man at the time of the Gardner job.

"So, all he knew was what he heard inside?"

"I think so. But that might be a lot."

This was going nowhere. These were just stray thoughts that Nancy had picked up and she hadn't processed any of it. Her comments struck me as reliable because she hadn't had the time to cook up a cover story. But I was unable to see where the tidbits I was getting might lead.

As we pulled into a surface lot near the morgue, Nancy grew quiet. Trips to the icebox were a professional hazard for some people in my business. I didn't use to be among them, but that was starting to change. I took her arm and walked her inside.

Heather, grim and in command of all she surveyed, was walking out as we were walking in. As soon as she recognized me, I could see her temperature rise. Then, she noticed the welt under my eye. It wasn't the first time she'd seen me bearing evidence of a fight.

"What happened to you?"

"Took a fall in the shower."

She appreciated the obvious deception. It obviated the need for small talk. Then, she took a look at Nancy.

"Who's this?"

"This is Nancy Herrick. Pam Herrick's sister."

I gestured down the hall to clarify the relationship.

"Is she your client?"

"No."

"Then, what are you doing here?"

I needed to come up with an answer that Heather would accept.

"Yes."

The last thing Heather needed was another homicide in her county and her patience was running thin. She turned to Nancy.

"Is this guy your lawyer or not?"

Nancy was a surface thinker, but she had a keen sense for where personal advantage lay.

"Of course he is," she said.

Heather huffed and got out of our way. She had no time for further discussion and all I wanted was to get back on the trail of my father.

Our footsteps echoed down a hallway of beige, glazed block, which reflected the bright light from the overhead lamps. A technician was still working on Pam, and when she saw us, she stepped back. Pam was on her back, under a sheet on a slab with an ID tag on her toe. The sheet was pulled up tight under her chin to conceal the brutal injury. Her face was pallid white, but someone had massaged her pretty features into an expression approaching repose.

Nancy took a breath and stepped forward. She took a brush out of her purse and brushed her sister's hair.

Then, she had her cry, said a heartfelt prayer, and kissed her sister on the forehead.

"Let's go," she said.

The cry helped, and she pulled herself together quickly. She was quiet for the first mile of the drive back to Crystal City, looking out the passenger window, humming softly to herself. I watched the landscape go by. Campaign signs had started to appear along the side of the road. Randy Hamburger's maroon and black yard signs were far more prevalent than the blue and white signs, reading "Heather!"

"There's a cemetery in Brockton. My parents are there."

She let the thought hang in the air. There would be paperwork and procedures and then the body would have to be shipped north. I was sure I knew more about this than Nancy did.

"I can make some calls."

"I'd appreciate it."

We were almost back before she spoke again.

"I guess it's back to Brockton for me."

I didn't respond.

"Or I could stay here with you."

"Yeah, I've thought about that. It might not be a great idea."

"For you or for me?"

"For you."

She laughed.

"You think I couldn't make do with a guy like you?"

I pulled up in front of the duplex and its weed-infested yard. On a gray, fall afternoon, it felt eerie, even for me.

"We'll talk about it. But not today."

She stared out the passenger window for what seemed like a long time.

"I can't stay in this house alone. Not tonight."

I understood.

"Okay. A couple of days."

We went inside and she filled a tattered, soft-sided suitcase with the things she thought she'd need. Then we gathered everything else she owned into a pair of card-board boxes. In the living room, with the suitcase hanging over her shoulder, she looked around and shook her head like someone trying to shake off a bad dream. She gave me her key and I promised to give it to Dan. By the time we left, there was no indication she had ever lived there.

It was a twenty-minute drive to my house, a little bungalow on a wooded lot in the Maywood section of the county. On the way, she had me stop at a drug store so she could get what she needed to get the blonde out of her hair. After that, neither of us broke the silence until we stepped inside my house.

"Can I get a drink?"

"Little early for that, don't you think?"

She shook her head with conviction.

"Not today."

The island that separated the kitchen from the living room served as a bar. I walked over and took stock, holding bottles up to the light to eyeball the contents.

"What are you drinking?"

"Dry Manhattan?"

"What's in a Dry Manhattan?"

"Take a glass, fill it with ice, three ounces of rye whiskey, one ounce of dry vermouth, a dash of bitters. And add a maraschino cherry if you have one."

"I've got the ice and the glass. We'll have to call out for everything else."

She smiled. She had a great, dimpled smile.

"I'll have the same thing as you."

I made her a bourbon and soda, which was as close as I could get to a Dry Manhattan. Then, I made her another one. And that's how it started.

"I'll put you in the guest room."

"No guest room for me. That's always the crummy bed."

She took my hand.

"Let's see what you've got."

It was easy to see what Dapper McNair saw in Nancy Herrick. And it was easy to see why she'd dropped him as soon as he got her out of Brockton. I could even understand why he was willing to accept it. She was a strong woman who called her own shots. What's not to like about that?

"Nancy, I've got some work to do."

"It's alright with me."

I got dressed and told her to make herself at home. By the way she looked around, I saw that she intended to do just that. In the meantime, there were a lot of questions I needed to answer, and most of them started with the whereabouts of Dapper McNair.

Chapter Twenty-Eight

Police Work

DP was seated at his long worktable, reading the local crime feed on his laptop. He looked up when I entered.

"Bad news in Crystal City," he said.

"Yeah."

"Pam Herrick. Any connection to Dan?"

"Yes. Her name was Pam, but Dan knew her as Yvonne."

I sat down across from him and filled him in quickly on Dapper's two pips scheme. It made sense to DP. Extra-legal schemes always did.

"Do the cops have any leads?"

"Not yet."

"McNair, you think?"

"Nancy doesn't believe it."

"Nancy? That's the sister?"

"Yeah. Irish Dan doesn't think so either. There's only one person I know with a reputation for strangling people."

DP nodded and tapped his nose.

"That seems likely. If he's out on his own, Pasquale's a very dangerous man."

"The police will take care of him," I said.

"What about Dapper?"

"What about him?"

"He's hip deep in it."

"The murder? Or the paintings?"

"Joth, the only thing I want is the paintings."

I nodded.

"That makes sense. You got some time this morning?"

DP smiled.

"Always for you."

He was dressed like a ninja in a black sweatshirt and black cargo pants. I nodded approvingly.

"Bring your lock picking kit."

"Where are we going?"

"We're going to break into a house."

On the drive to Crystal City, I explained the situation to DP as I understood it, sparing no details. He took some time thinking it through.

"If Felipe killed Pam Herrick, it wasn't a random killing. He was after something."

"I already thought of that. It's got to tie back to Dapper."

"Maybe. But if it goes to Dapper, it might go to your dad."

I shook my head.

"I don't think so. Somebody's got their facts confused and I think it's Nancy."

"What did she tell you?"

"For one thing, she thinks my father's a musician. Believe me, nothing could be further from the truth."

DP's ears perked up.

"A musician? How did that come up?"

"She said that my father and Dapper were in a band before he went to prison. My dad didn't play anything but the ponies."

"That doesn't necessarily mean he was playing in the band. Maybe he was the manager."

I shook my head.

"No. I'd have known about it."

"But why northern Virginia? He couldn't get gigs for Pam up north?"

"Nancy said he had a line on something down here."

"Nancy said that?"

"Yup. But she's used to giving people the answers she thinks they want to hear. I don't think she knows what she's talking about."

I parked around the corner from McNair's place. DP studied it like a cat burglar while I called Dapper's cell one more time.

"Nobody's home."

"The car's here," he said.

"I know. It's been here all morning."

McNair didn't strike me as the kind of guy who went anywhere on foot.

I banged loudly on the front door, waited, then banged again, even louder. I listened for any sound coming from inside but heard nothing. Then I checked the door. Locked. DP was already unzipping his lock picking kit.

"If anybody comes," I said, "we're checking to make sure Dan's tenant is okay."

He flashed his crooked smile at me.

"Relax, Joth. Nobody ever comes."

Dan didn't invest much money in securing his properties. There was a five-pin cylinder lock in the door handle. After glancing over his shoulder, DP raked it quickly and turned the knob with the tension wrench. He pushed it open.

Once inside the house, the first thing I noticed was exactly what I was looking for: the Flinck that hung over the mantlepiece and the Manet that had hung beside it were gone. I swore vehemently, which caught DP's attention.

"He's flown the coop and he took the art."

DP shook his head and waved a hand at the collection of clothes and personal objects strewn about the living room. I hadn't even noticed. Someone had ransacked the place.

I busied myself looking in closets and under furniture for the Manet and the Flinck, but DP went immediately upstairs. I was poking around in the hall closet when I heard his voice.

"Joth, you better get up here."

The master bedroom was at the top of the stairs. DP was standing beside the bed. I shrunk back from the sight.

"How long has he been dead?"

"Long enough to start stinking. Open that window, will you?"

A heavy smell like rotting fruit pervaded the room and I opened the window and stood there for a moment filling my lungs with fresh air. Two dead bodies in less than 24 hours was a lot to stomach.

I walked over and stood beside DP. McNair's skin had already begun to take on a grayish pallor. One arm was draped across the bedspread. DP lifted it, testing its rigidity.

"Ten hours. Maybe less," he said.

"So, last night?"

"Yeah. Around midnight, give or take."

DP reached down and shut Dapper's eyes with a thumb and forefinger. Dapper was between the sheets with a bedspread up to his chin. Without his wig, he was bald as an egg and his face was bloated. Death disfigures a man quickly.

"What do you think? I said. "He had cirrhosis of the liver. We know that. He felt badly so he came upstairs to lie down?"

"Maybe."

"Cirrhosis of the liver can kill you, right?"

"Yes, but not like this. It's not sudden, like if you have a heart attack."

I tended to think that the simplest answer was the best, but I could tell by DP's expression that he was sifting through other possibilities. He pulled down the sheet and bedspread. Dapper was dressed in a pair of silk pajamas, but we both noticed bruising around his throat.

"You think somebody strangled him?"

"Looks like it," said DP.

If so, both he and Pam had been strangled, their bodies found in different places, but within close proximity in time and location. It wasn't a coincidence.

"Okay, so Pam . . ."

He let the thought trail off.

"Nancy said she ran errands for him. That was part of the deal."

"What kind of errand is she going to be running at midnight?"

In an effort to answer his own question, DP unclipped a penlight from his belt and used the butt end to carefully push around the items on the crowded side table: drink glasses, cigarette butts in an ashtray, medications and prescription bottles and a half-eaten ham and cheese sandwich.

"Look at this."

Among the debris was a crumpled paper bag. A receipt was stapled to it, time stamped at 11:53 the previous night. DP carefully picked it up. The bag had been opened and inside were several over-the-counter medications and a prescription refill for something called Ursodiol.

"Recognize that?"

"Yes," said DP. "It's commonly used to treat cirrhosis."

He pulled out a handkerchief and turned the orange-tinted prescription bottles on the table so that we could read the labels. One of them read Ursodiol and it was empty. Although the bag was open, all the containers in it were still sealed.

"Dapper called Pam," I said. "She made a midnight run to get medication for him. The killer happened to see her in the CVS and followed her here?"

DP shook his head.

"I don't think so. Look at the address of the CVS. If he wants to kill her, there are plenty of spots to accost her between here and there, especially on a foggy night."

"He was after Dapper?"

"He must have thought she'd lead him to him," he said.

"And she did."

DP sat down and put his chin in his hand.

"So, how do you figure it?"

"I'm betting she got a call from Dapper at about eleven. She went out and got his meds. That's what she was supposed to do, right?"

DP looked at me for my assessment and I nodded. I was following his logic.

"Right. Don't forget, she hasn't got a car," I said. "To get to the CVS, buy what she needs and get over here, that takes at least forty-five minutes. But she's the good sister. She'll do it and won't complain."

"So, who's the killer?" I said.

"Somebody who wanted the paintings and was willing to kill to get them."

"Pasquale, you think?"

"Pasquale means Jimmie."

DP shook his head.

"Jimmie knew Dapper had the paintings and he knew where he lived. Flambeau wouldn't have needed to follow Pam to find him."

He went back to the cluttered side table and picked up Dapper's phone. He held it over the dead man to open it with facial recognition, then tapped the phone function and accessed the call log.

He read off a seven-digit number beginning with Boston's familiar 978 area code.

"What time?"

"Five after eleven."

"That tracks."

I watched as he swiped through to Settings to reset the Password.

"What do you think? 'Dapper'."

"That seems appropriate."

He made the change and tossed the phone to me. I slipped it into my pocket. We both knew we were tampering with evidence at a murder scene, but you take your edges where you can. We were too far in to stop now.

There was a chair in the bedroom, covered with un-folded laundry. I dropped into it.

"You saw the downstairs, Joth. It's a wreck. Whoever killed him was ransacking the place, looking for something. That's when she walked in."

"Could be."

"I'm guessing he strangled her downstairs and put the bag with the meds up here to muddy the waters."

He looked at me to measure my expression. I nodded.

"It was a foggy night. He dumped her body off Fern Street."

"That follows. Last question," DP said. "Who's *he*?"

"Somebody who wanted those paintings; the Manet and the Flinck."

The only person I knew who fit that description was Jimmie Flambeau, but Jimmie did not do his own killing.

DP noticed a pair of jeans hanging on a hook on the back of the door. He reached into the back pocket and pulled out a brown leather wallet, held it between two fingers to avoid leaving prints and tossed it on the bed. I approached and leaned over his shoulder. Working carefully, he emptied the meager contents on the bed and pushed through it. The wallet contained just over two hundred dollars in cash, several credit cards and a Massachusetts driver's license in the name Nancy had given me: David Taylor. It was a picture of a much younger man with a mullet.

"Take about a quarter century of hard living off that face and what have you got?"

"That's not him, Joth. Close enough to pass a casual inspection, but it's a different person."

I looked again, more carefully. The dead man's nose and chin didn't quite match those of the person in the photo. Now I understood why he wore the rusty wig. But no matter how much younger the man pictured on the license looked; the corpse on the bed had never been that man.

"I'll tell you one thing, DP. Whoever killed him took those two paintings."

DP nodded, as if he'd already thought of that. He gathered the contents of the wallet, carefully replaced them inside, and, after wiping his prints, put it back in the jeans pocket. He sat down in the chair I had occupied a few minutes before. He licked his lips and looked away from me. Then, he took another glance at the body.

"We better call an ambulance."

He pulled out his cellphone, checked the time on his watch and made the call to 911. After he hung up, he looked at me.

"Who killed him, Joth?"

"Who do we know who strangles people? Pasquale."

"Joth, whoever killed McNair wanted the paintings. But Flambeau knew where to find them. There was no reason to bring in Pasquale on a job like that."

He sighed.

"You're not looking at the connections, Joth."

"What connections?"

"Look, he cased the museum. He looks like the sketch of one of the robbers, and he may have the Vermeer."

"What are you talking about?"

"McNair came down here looking for him, didn't he? Joth, your father has *The Concert*. Or at least he had it. That's what Dapper was talking about. Not *a* concert. *The* Concert. And now, Dapper's dead."

This was the first time DP had ever made me angry.

"What are you saying?"

"Joth, I'm only asking you to look at the facts."

"There aren't any facts."

"Why do you think he took the finial? You liked it. He took it for you. Joth. It all adds up. It was your father and this man who called himself Dapper McNair who hit the Gardner that night."

I raised a hand.

"Be careful what comes out of your mouth, DP."

"I know this is not easy. I'm just asking you to think about it. You can find your own answers."

"I already know the answer to that, and when I find my dad, you'll know it, too."

DP looked at me.

"Whatever you say, Joth."

DP was often right, and while he might not have been right about this, he was at least heading in the right direction. There weren't a lot of people who might have taken those paintings and I was refusing to even consider one of the most obvious suspects. Or was I? DP took Dapper's phone because he thought it might lead to the paintings. But that was also why I was hanging on to it.

I sat in the chair and waited for the police to arrive. Five minutes later, we heard the sirens. Arlington cops travel in packs. Two squad cars accompanied an ambulance, with two cops in each car. We'd left the door unlocked and DP went to the top of the stairs when he heard them come in.

"Up here," he said.

They spread out like special forces. Two cops led the way up, while two EMTs in navy blue coveralls collapsed the stretcher, then manhandled it up the stairs. The second pair of cops secured the first floor before following up the stairs a few minutes later. One of the officers in the first pair put his hands on his hips.

"I guess they're giving PI licenses to anybody these days."

The nameplate below the officer's badge read Charles Hixon. I didn't recognize him, but DP did. He winced but didn't speak.

Hixon's partner was Jerome Flayberry. He stepped up to the bed and gave the corpse a quick visual examination. He looked up, recognized me, and raised a hand in acknowledgement. When a third officer, Jake Spotswood, came in from downstairs, he and DP exchanged nods.

"What happened?"

"We found him like this, Jake," DP said.

"How'd you happen to be here?"

"Doing a wellness check for the landlord."

Hixon spoke up.

"Since when does Dan Crowley send a lawyer and a private dick to do a wellness check for him?"

"He did today," said DP.

Hixon turned and stared at him.

"How'd you get in?"

"Dan gave us a key."

Hixon didn't believe DP, who made no effort to convince him. We all knew that Dan would back us up, but we were off on the wrong foot with Hixon.

"What time did you get here?"

"I don't know," said DP. "I didn't look at my watch. Ten minutes ago?"

He looked at me and I nodded.

"You touch anything?"

"Nope. As soon as we saw he was dead, I made the call."

One of the EMT's completed a quick examination, then huddled with Hixon and Flayberry. Hixon crooked a finger at Spotswood.

"Escort these two gentlemen out of here."

He turned to DP and me.

"You can expect to be called at the inquest, when you'll be under oath."

DP let a small smile turn up the edges of his mouth. "Sure."

Spotswood followed us down the stairs. He knew DP, but he didn't share Hixon's animus. At the bottom of the stairs, DP spoke up quietly.

"What do you think happened?"

"I know what the EMT thinks. Somebody strangled him."

"That's the easy part," said DP. "Any suspects?"

"Yeah. A guy named Felipe Pasquale. You know him?"

"Heard of him. I thought he was out of town."

"He surfaced this week. Got into a dust up over at Willard's."

"The guy who walked out of jail?"

Spotswood nodded.

"Yeah. He would have strangled that guy if Raighne Youngblood hadn't interfered, so we got an MO. He probably strangled that girl this morning, too. He's priority number one. If he's in Arlington, we'll find him."

If Felipe Pasquale was still in the area, a lot of people were in danger. I was just one of them.

Chapter Twenty-Nine

A Story That Fits

The next stop was Riding Time. DP and I had a pair of related murders on our hands and the walk gave us a chance to talk. By the time we arrived, we'd developed a take on the facts that would keep us all out of hot water and buy time to put the missing pieces together.

It was lunch hour on a weekday by then, a busy time for Dan. The place was as crowded and as animated as a carnival midway. Cigarette smoke and a heavy backbeat hung in the air. A slender woman, known as Crisp, worked the cage in the back in a G string and pasties. A tall brunette, named Lynx, paused on the main stage to allow a businessman in a cheap suit to tuck a portrait of Alexander Hamilton into her garter.

We pushed our way through the crowd toward Dan at the bar. He was used to me appearing at all hours, but when he saw DP at my side, he walked quickly toward us.

"You got that look, Joth."

"Can we sit?"

With the promise of free beer, he shooed a pair of younger patrons out of a booth and we sat down.

"Coffee?"

I nodded.

"Tea for me."

Dan snapped his fingers and repeated the order to a redheaded woman with a mermaid tattooed on the pale skin above her breasts. I gave it a moment, then sighed for effect, which caught Dan's attention.

"More news, Joth?"

"Yeah, and it's not good."

"Eva? The other pip?"

"Her name's Nancy, and she's safe."

He took a heavy breath.

"It's Dapper McNair, Dan. He's been strangled."

He processed this information with a nod, then stared at me, waiting for more.

"We found him in the place you rented to him. He's been dead since last night. The police are there now."

Dan nodded.

"It's a grim day."

"It is."

The waitress brought the coffee and tea. Dan recognized that the events of the night before could ensnare him, but he had the ability to summon a stoical focus when circumstances required it.

"Is this related to what happened to Yvonne?"

"You mean Pam? Yeah, I think so."

I looked at DP and he nodded. Dan liked to be given a game plan, and he was good at sticking to it.

"The police will be here soon. They'll be asking the same question."

"And others," said DP.

"Like what?"

"You're going to have to tell them Pam was staying in one of your places," I said. "But you can drop the whole Albanian royal family nonsense."

"But it's . . ."

"It doesn't matter, Dan."

DP nodded.

"They're going to figure out that she was hooked up with McNair, and it's okay for you to know that, too."

"And the sister?"

"The sister is Nancy," I said. "The dead girl is Pam."

Dan nodded.

DP spoke up.

"When you identified Pam's body, did you say anything about the sister?"

"No."

"You sure?"

"I'm always sure what I say to cops and it's as little as possible."

DP and I exchanged glances.

"Okay, Dan," I said. "This is important. You don't know anybody named Eva or Nancy. There was only one girl. Only Pam. Got it?"

"Sounds like you don't want Nancy talking to the police."

"*You* don't want her talking to the police, Dan. Dead men and women tell no tales and Pam and Dapper are both dead. I'm going to try to keep Nancy out of it, but if asked, she's going to say she and her sister came down here with McNair trying to help Pam make it in the music business. But as far as you knew, there was only the one. Just Pam. She was a concert level pianist and McNair fashioned himself as her manager. He talked you into putting him and Pam up for a short period of time while he lined up some work for her."

To his credit, Dan Crowley didn't blame the Herrick sisters for their part in Dapper McNair's scam. After all, it was just money and Dan never let money get in the way.

"Yeah, that's it," said Dan.

"He was going to cut you in for a percentage in return for the free rent. Nothing in writing, of course."

"Of course."

"You ever hear him talk about music, about a band, anything like that?"

Dan had a nice way of latching onto a storyline and making it his own.

"Yeah, I did. That was one of the things he wanted to do: line up a concert or two. Yvonne, or Pam, really could play, you know."

DP and I exchanged glances and DP spoke up.

"Don't overdo it, Dan."

"No, It's the truth. He had big plans for that girl."

I wasn't sure if Dan was repeating what Dapper had told him or if he was making it up as he went along, but it didn't matter. Dapper had met with Emily Davison, but that relationship hadn't progressed enough for her to gather any inconvenient facts. There was nobody left to worry about.

"Okay. Keep it simple. When in doubt, tell them what Dapper or Pam told you. There's no one left to contradict any of that."

"I get it. How much time does Eva, or Nancy, need to get her stuff out of there?"

"Eva? Never heard of her."

I looked at DP and he nodded. We got up and shook hands with Dan. Cops like simple answers, and I thought this would be the end of it. The police would tie the murders together and hang them both on Pasquale. They'd never stumble onto Nancy at all, and DP and I would be free to chase the paintings. Or so I thought.

Chapter Thirty

Happy Birthday

When I got home, I found Nancy in the kitchen, but she wasn't dressed to make dinner. She had successfully gotten the blonde out of her hair and the dye had done her no favors. She was one of those olive-skinned women who looked much better as a brunette. She also looked great in brown leather pants and a denim work shirt, tied at the waist over a lacy green cotton blouse. She was dressed for effect and it was working.

"What have you been doing all day?"

"Well, I walked down to the supermarket. Then, I cleaned this place up a little bit."

I tended to keep my house in much the same state that Nancy and her sister had maintained Dan's Crystal City duplex. I hadn't even noticed.

"Maybe we can arrange some tender loving care for your face tonight. Do you have a wok?"

"A what?"

"A wok. I was going to make stir fry. Do you like stir fry?"

"I don't know. I've never had it."

There was a small table and two chairs under the kitchen window where I took most of my meals. I sat down while she poked around until she found a large frying pan under the stove.

"Well. I can make a frying pan do."

"What's for dessert?"

"Oh, I never make dessert," she said.

She caught herself and quickly improvised.

"I mean, not unless I'm making pastry for a big group."

"Yeah. Who came up with this pastry chef scam? You or Dapper?"

She looked at me for a long moment.

"It might have been me."

"That's what I figured. You're smarter than he was. Now, I want to hear about the big scam you and Dapper cooked up."

Nancy sat down across from me and made sure I had a good look at her. Her sister's body was still in the morgue, but Nancy was cool and focused, as if she'd spent all afternoon preparing for the moment of confrontation she knew was coming.

"You mean the music? That was Dapper's idea."

"No. He didn't know how good Pam was. You told him."

She shrugged and checked her nails.

"So what? It was true."

"People don't come to Arlington, Virginia to break into the music business."

"Well, David did."

"But that's not what happened at all, is it? He came down here because he thought he could get his hands on twenty million dollars in the form of a painting by Johannes Vermeer. You started sleeping with him so that he'd take you along. Your sister, too. I'm willing to bet you're the one who came up with the Wonderlace sisters. It was perfect. All you had to do was watch TV all day while he tracked down my father. And now, you think I can get my hands on it. So, you traded up, didn't you?"

She didn't even blink.

"Dapper never meant anything to me. A tired old man. But you and me. That's different."

"No, it's not."

She wet her lips.

"I've got two months and my sister's life invested in this. I'm here to stay, Joth."

"Why not? There's no one else to split it with."

"That's a mean thing to say."

"Is it? Or is it the truth?"

She primped her hair.

"Where'd you hide the paintings, Nancy?"

"What paintings?"

"The Flinck and the Manet. The two paintings that Dapper took from the Gardner all those years ago."

"I don't know what you're talking about."

"Come on, Nancy. Of course, you do. He brought them down from Massachusetts and you were right there in the car. It's a long drive. It had to come up."

"It didn't."

"Okay, enough with the easy stuff. Dapper didn't call your sister last night. He called you."

She shook her head emphatically.

"No."

"I've seen his phone, Nancy. I recognized your number because Dan gave it to me. Pam may have been nicer, but you were the girlfriend. Dapper always called you. He called you at five past eleven last night because he needed medicine. You passed the job on to your sister, like you always do. When she didn't come back, you went to Dapper's, looking for her. You didn't find Pam, but you found a dead body. Then, you did what I'd expect you to do. You took the two paintings that were hanging on his wall."

"That's nuts!"

She looked legitimately startled. I'd hit on something, but I wasn't sure what.

"If you hand me your phone, I'll bet you the value of the Manet that it will show that you called your sister right after Dapper called you."

When she failed to find an answer, I saw that I was right.

"Where were you last night? Out with a guy?"

"Yeah, I was out. So what?"

That stung me more than I wanted to admit. But that wasn't what this was about. I stood up and leaned over the table.

"I want the paintings, Nancy."

"I don't have them! Use your head. Where would I have put them at one o'clock in the morning?"

I put something on the table where she could see it.

"What this?"

"It's a bus ticket to Boston. I'm sure a resourceful girl like you can find your way to Brockton from there."

She stood up and glared at me.

"Alright, I'm a person who's gotten through life by grabbing at opportunities. You figured that out. Bravo. But I didn't take the paintings. Not because I wouldn't have, but I wasn't there last night."

"What was his name?"

"What was whose name?"

"The guy you were with last night."

"Her name, you mean. Her name was Sarah."

She had finally surprised me. I looked at her carefully and measured the malice in her dark, hooded eyes. I never really thought she'd taken the paintings, but I wished she had. It would have made it a lot easier for me to put her on that bus.

***

The next morning, I got a call from Jimmie, who had never been very far out of my mind, even in the midst of all the chaos. I assumed he had some of the answers I was looking for and I was determined to shake them out of him.

"How's your face?"

It was an unusually considerate question coming from him, but I was feeling unusually pugnacious, and I stepped away from the normal courtesies.

"Better than yours."

He skipped over the insult. He could afford to.

"I want you to drop the Ish McGriff matter."

"That deadbeat tenant I've been chasing for the rent he owes you? What? He paid?"

"He paid enough."

It took me a moment to process that. As far as I knew, anything less than the full amount had never been good enough for Jimmie Flambeau. So, why was he compromising with Ish?

"You want me to drop it?"

"Yeah. Just forget you ever had it. Send me your bill and I'll pay it right away."

"Okay."

I was on a monthly retainer, so Jimmie didn't owe me anything. A man who counts nickels like Flambeau was aware of that.

"You want me to send you a bill for my time?'

"What, are you going deaf?"

"Anything else?"

"I'll let you know if something comes up."

An hour later, I was still processing Jimmie's unexplained generosity when DP showed up with a somber expression and started pacing around my office.

"Okay DP, let's have it."

"I just got some news over the police band. Felipe Pasquale was killed in a shoot-out with the police."

Jimmie was quickly forgotten.

"When?"

"This morning. It's just in. That's all I know."

I sucked in my breath and exhaled hard.

"That should take a load off your mind," DP said.

"It should take a load off everyone's mind. There were a lot of people in his crosshairs."

"That's true, Joth, except now we'll never know for sure who killed Dapper and the girl."

"Are you kidding? Pasquale was a bad dude and he's dead. The cop who killed him ought to get a medal."

"I guess it's just a matter of how closely people want to look at the evidence."

"All that matters is that Pasquale's dead, DP. You know that nobody will be asking questions about why or how."

But something was troubling DP.

"If I am, others will, too."

"Then, you have to stop asking."

I chuckled and he nodded to acknowledge the dig on his way out the door.

I hadn't spoken to Heather since our brief exchange in the morgue. Now, I had some news to share that wasn't complicated by marital discord, compromising video, or the complexities of renewing our romance.

I picked up the phone and called her.

"I heard Pasquale is dead of what for him were natural causes."

I thought I heard a chuckle.

"It's not a laughing matter," she said.

"But he's dead?"

"Oh yeah, he's dead. One bullet right through the ticker."

"What happened?"

"The investigative division tracked him to an apartment in Rosslyn, one of those low-rise, brick set-ups right down the street from here. Two teams of two cops each and a deputy driving the meat wagon went to pick him up."

I tried to picture it.

"Two officers covering the door around back and two serving the warrant?"

"Yeah, plus the deputy."

"He put up a fight?"

"That's a strange question for you to be asking. Of course."

"Well, Heather, this ought to be a good thing for your campaign: a very bad man taken down by officers in the line of duty."

"I hope so. The public tends to trust deputies a little more than the boys in blue when there's a shooting, but cowboy justice is never good for a prosecutor."

My ears perked up.

"The deputy shot him?"

"Yeah."

"What's his name?"

I asked, but I already knew.

They'd put Ish on administrative suspension, pending an internal affairs investigation, and I knew the investigation would clear him. They always do.

I pulled up the file and jotted down Ish McGriff's South Arlington address. Then, I got in my car. I wasn't ready to declare Ish as Jimmie's new henchman, but the connection between Felipe's death and Jimmie's sudden decision to forgive Ish's rent was too obvious to ignore.

***

In north Arlington, most of the modest brick ramblers that had characterized the county's residential inventory in the decades after the Cold War had been renovated into million-dollar homes or knocked down entirely to create space for the statement homes that characterized modern and affluent Arlington, but south of Arlington Boulevard, where the prefixes changed from north to south, much of the old status quo still prevailed.

McGriff's place was one among a faceless row of Monopoly style houses distinguishable only by their color. There were no curbs or sidewalks, and in yard after yard, patchy grass ran down to the street. There was one exception: a yard of green, freshly mowed grass in front of a house of recently painted white brick. The shutters were off the windows and stacked up neatly on sawhorses, as if ready for painting. I checked the address again and pulled up in front.

As I knocked, I heard a noise inside, like furniture being moved, and then noticed a subtle change in light that showed someone was at the peephole. A moment later, the door opened.

Ish was dressed in a gray sweatshirt and jeans. He wore a yellow bandana around his neck and a freshly splattered painter's cap. The roller he held in his right hand dripped white paint into a pan. He gave me the sort of grin you'd share with a familiar friend.

"You caught me at kind of a bad time, Joth."

"Yeah?"

I pushed past him. Ish raised his eyebrows, but he was too surprised to object or resist.

There was an aluminum step-ladder in the middle of the room. He was painting the ceiling. Tarps had been spread across the carpet and clear plastic covered the furniture, leaving no place to sit, but I perched on the edge of a covered chair.

"I wasn't expecting to see you," he said.

"Paperwork mix-up, huh?"

"That does happen, you know. I called you when it did."

"Yeah, and I guess you volunteered to drive the meat wagon?"

I'd reached the limit of Ish's patience.

"Hey, man, what's this all about? I didn't invite you here."

It was always a mistake to get angry. I knew that. But that knowledge had never stopped me before and it didn't stop me now.

"And now you're getting free rent?"

"What are you talking about."

"Isn't that the deal you struck with Flambeau?"

"No, it's not the deal."

"Why don't you tell me what it is?"

I expected Ish to be intimidated by this direct assault, but he wasn't.

"It's none of your damn business."

"I'm making it my business."

I could see him weighing the prospect of a physical confrontation and I'm sure I looked crazy enough to cause one. He smiled to himself and nodded as he placed the roller in the pan and put it on the tarp.

"Okay. Me and the landlord made a business arrangement."

"And what's that?"

"Simple. I fix up his properties. On my time and at my expense. When I'm done, I move on. He gets to charge a higher rent to the next tenant, and I fix up the next place the same way. And, that's how I pay my rent. It's a fair deal."

"Nice try. Flambeau doesn't care about these properties. He's going to sell them to a developer. And you'd do the work anyway. You told me that in my office."

He wagged his finger.

"You heard wrong, Mr. Proctor."

I wondered for a moment if Flambeau had hooked Pasquale in the same way, but I doubted it. Felipe was just a thug. Ish was much smarter, and that made him much more dangerous.

He cocked his head to look at me. I could feel the arrogance of a cop who knows he can get away with just about anything.

"A bad man is dead, Mr. Proctor. Nobody's gonna mourn him. Without him, we live in a better place. You doubt that?"

I didn't answer.

"And, you were right, Mr. Proctor. It's good to get this behind me."

He picked up the roller pan, climbed the stepladder, and resumed rolling the ceiling as if I wasn't there. I let myself out.

***

I should have waited and given time for the news of Pasquale's shooting to sink in. But I didn't. Instead, I called Flambeau from my car on the way back to the office. Helen fielded the call. It was a measure of my growing status with Jimmie that she didn't put me on hold while she checked his availability. Instead, she told me to come right over.

It was a cold afternoon in October and the high-rise office buildings created a tunnel for the blustery wind that rushed down Wilson Boulevard. Helen had a warm welcome for me, as if I was the good kid in her fifth-grade class.

"Go right in."

She reached under the desk and dropped the bolt to Jimmie's inner office.

I'd been around long enough to understand that Helen's daily mood usually reflected Jimmie's, so I knew I'd caught Jimmie on a good day. Felipe's demise had a way of making everybody feel better.

Jimmie was wearing a dark suit, a white shirt, and a black necktie and looked up from his desk as I walked in.

"Virginia's giving three points at Carolina Saturday."

I sat down.

"Yeah? Is that a tip?"

"It's a favor. Take it."

"Carolina's quarterback get somebody pregnant?"

He didn't laugh. Money wasn't funny.

"That'd be worth a lot more than three points."

I thought back to Jimmie's promise of a bonus after I'd brought Mitch Tressler's account current. Maybe this was the way he paid off the people who got in his good graces. Why not? He might get me hooked at the same time. Then again, maybe I already was.

"I heard Ish McGriff is the guy who shot Pasquale."

"Is he?"

"Last time I saw you in a tie you were at the wake of a friend of mine."

He nodded and tried to make it look sincere.

"Holly Sullivan."

Holly owed him money. A lot of people owed Jimmie money, and a lot of them ended up dead.

"There's another wake today," said Jimmie. "A long-time associate of mine has been killed and I feel an obligation to go. Funerals are for those left behind."

It took me a moment to understand that he was talking about Pasquale.

"This associate of yours killed Nick Grimes."

"He did that in a fit of passion. That can be forgiven."

"And I don't know how many others."

"Hate the sin, love the sinner," said Jimmie. "Didn't the nuns teach you that in Sunday School?"

His hypocrisy astonished me, and I was about to tell him so when I remembered *Chez Tortoni*. I turned, expecting to see it hanging in its spot above the safe, but it wasn't there. When I turned back toward him, Flambeau was smiling.

"What happened to that painting? The Manet?"

"I told you, the guy took it back."

I was mystified. Wasn't this the reason he had ordered Pasquale to kill Dapper?

After the pause that followed, Jimmie returned to the subject of the funeral.

"You ought to go yourself," he said. "It would do you good."

I had finally reached a point when my anger and confusion were undermining my purpose. I had to get out of there before I did something stupid.

"See you around, Jimmie."

I got up and left.

***

When I got back to the office, DP was at Marie's desk and by the look of things they were discussing the commonplace business issues of the day. I stepped between them and grabbed DP by the elbow.

"I need to talk to you."

He took a long look at my face and nodded. I led him into my office and shut the door.

"You better sit down for this."

I waited until he did.

"Ish McNair is the deputy who killed Felipe Pasquale."

DP whistled.

"Not only that, just this morning Jimmie Flambeau told me to stop pursing Ish for unpaid rent."

"And you don't believe in coincidences."

"You want to know what I believe? Jimmie is grooming a new enforcer."

"Is it that easy?"

"It might be for McGriff."

I gave DP time to process this news dump, hoping he would break the silence that followed with a new insight, but there was too much to digest. We were still brooding on opposite sides of the desk when Marie came in, carrying a package covered in brown wrapping paper and tied up with twine.

"This just came for you, Mr. Proctor."

She put it in the middle of the desk.

"A messenger dropped it off. He said you've been expecting it."

I hefted it.

"Heavy."

DP stood up, his face showing his usual curiosity for all things peculiar.

"Who wraps a package like that anymore?"

There was no return address, just the name "Joth Proctor" written across it in block letters.

"Nobody I know."

"Let's find out."

I took out my pocketknife, but DP reached out and restrained my arm.

"Be careful."

He saw something I didn't.

"Why?"

"No address. No return address. This doesn't feel right."

I shrugged and cut the twine, then used the edge of the blade to rip off the paper, exposing a box of corrugated cardboard.

"Should I be worried about this?"

DP grunted. He didn't know either, but I was feeling reckless. I pulled open the top of the box. What I found inside weakened my knees, and DP's too. My hands were shaking as I took it out and placed it on the desk. It was a gilded eagle about ten inches tall. Its wings were spread and it glared as if it were angry at DP and me.

We both knew what it was. We'd been looking at pictures of it for the better part of a month. It was the bronze eagle from the French Grenadiers battle standard that had been stolen from the Gardner so many years ago.

DP took a big breath. It took a lot to leave him speechless.

"The finial from the Gardner heist," I said.

I looked into the bottom of the box.

"There's something else."

I took out a plain white envelope. Inside was a card with a stylized drawing of a man in what's known as a capotain, a tall, crowned hat with a buckle on the front; the kind my Puritan ancestors would have worn. There was a speech bubble emanating from the man's mouth.

"Remember, your birthday lasts as long as it takes for your family to remember it."

That's all the card said. It was unsigned, but it didn't matter. The only remaining member of my family was my father.

I sat down. DP gave me some space. I knew I had made a deal with the devil, but I was no longer sure who the devil was.

About the Author

James V. Irving was born and raised in Gloucester, Massachusetts. He is a graduate of the University of Virginia (UVA), where he majored in English. He holds a law degree from the College of William and Mary and is a member of the bars of Virginia, Maryland, the District of Columbia and Massachusetts.

After completing his undergraduate studies at UVA, Mr. Irving spent two years employed as a private detective in Northern Virginia, where he pursued wayward spouses, located skips, investigated insurance claims and handled criminal investigations. In his early years as a lawyer, he practiced criminal law, which along with his investigative experience and trial work, informs this fictional account of Joth Proctor, an under-employed criminal defense lawyer faced with spiraling personal and professional challenges which put his livelihood, and ultimately his personal freedom, at risk.

Upcoming New Release!

FRIEND IN THE BULLSEYE
BOOK 5
A JOTH PROCTOR FIXER MYSTERY
BY
JAMES V. IRVING

After the dramatic death of Heather's political rival, all eyes focus on the person who benefits most. Joth is committed to clearing Heather's name, but when other clients and friends find themselves in the crosshairs, Joth faces conflicts that muddy the investigative waters. Truth is elusive where motives are mixed.

For more information
visit: www.SpeakingVolumes.us

  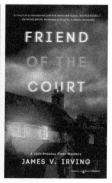

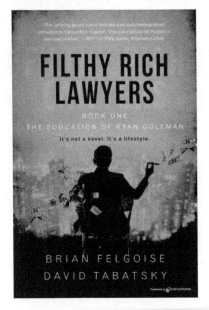

Now Available!

STEPHEN H. MORIARTY

"An ex-prosecutor, Moriarty knows his way around the
courthouse and the courtroom, and he brings both alive with
a thrilling story and memorable characters."
—James Irving, author of the *Joth Proctor* Mystery Series.

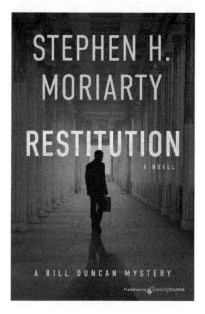

For more information
visit: www.SpeakingVolumes.us

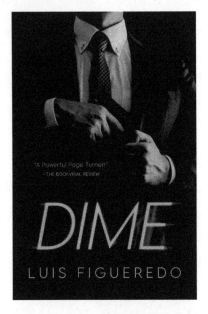

Lightning Source UK Ltd.
Milton Keynes UK
UKHW041001010323
417851UK00001B/120